A Tale of Two Abbeys

The third Sherborne Medieval mystery

Featuring Matthias Barton.

By

Rosie Lear

Grosvenor House
Publishing Limited

The right of Rosie Lear to be identified as the author of this
work has been asserted in accordance with Section 78
of the Copyright, Designs and Patents Act 1988

The book cover is copyright to Rosie Lear
The book cover design by Neil Pockett

This book is published by
Grosvenor House Publishing Ltd
Link House
140 The Broadway, Tolworth, Surrey, KT6 7HT.
www.grosvenorhousepublishing.co.uk

This book is a work of fiction but based upon real-life historical events
and characters. The story is a product of the author's imagination and
should not be construed as true.

A CIP record for this book
is available from the British Library

ISBN 978-1-78623-576-3

For my brothers, Neil and David
And my sister Alison
From the leader of the pack, with love.

My thanks to Bob Chimley for the maps.
Thanks also to John Porter, for permission to use
the map of Gillingham Forest.

www.rosielearbooks.com

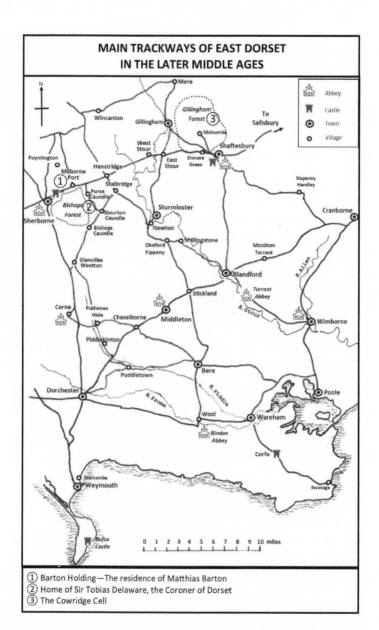

MAIN TRACKWAYS OF EAST DORSET
IN THE LATER MIDDLE AGES

Mere

Wincanton

Gillingham
Gillingham Forest ③
Motcombe

To Salisbury

West Stour

Shaftesbury

Poyntington

Milborne Port ①

Henstridge

East Stour
Enmore Green

Stalbridge

Purse Caundle

Bishops Forest ②

Stourton Caundle

Sherborne

Bishops Caundle

Sturminster

Newton

Sixpenny Handley

Cranborne

Okeford Fippeny

Shillingstone

Glanvilles Wootton

Monkton Tarrant

R. Allen

Blandford

Cerne

Piddletren thide

Cheselborne

Stickland

Tarrant Abbey

R. Stour

Middleton

Wimborne

Piddlehinton

Bere

Puddletown

Dorchester

R. Frome

R. Piddle

Poole

Wool

Wareham

Bindon Abbey

Corfe

Melcombe
Weymouth

Rufus Castle

Swanage

| Abbey |
| Castle |
| Town |
| Village |

0 1 2 3 4 5 6 7 8 9 10 miles

① Barton Holding—The residence of Matthias Barton
② Home of Sir Tobias Delaware, the Coroner of Dorset
③ The Cowridge Cell

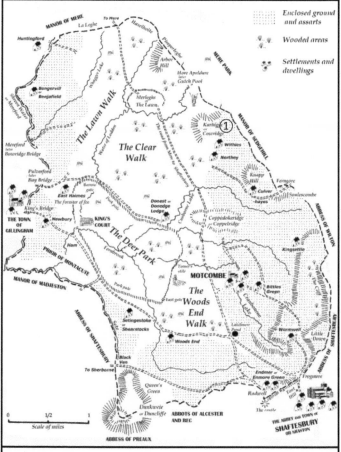

THE FOREST OF GILLINGHAM
IN THE LATER MIDDLE AGES
With King's Court and the Deer Park

© John Porter 2013

① Location of the Cowridge Cell

Shaftesbury – 1438

Brother John fell to his knees in the dust of his chapel, trembling at the memories of the sights he had witnessed. Such horror...such bloodshed.....so much violence.

He hoped never to see such things again. Whom could he tell? He was alone in this place. He closed his eyes. He would tell God, - there was no-one else to tell.

But first he must attend to the woman he had carried here...she was still alive, though badly injured. He had left her a short distance away when his feeble strength gave out....revived a little now, he fetched his great cloak and using his stick to steady his feet, he returned to the edge of the forest. He was relieved to find her still there, lying on the grass where he had left her. Carefully he spread his cloak out and rolled her inert body onto it, heeding little the blood stains which would remain. With this extra assistance, he began to drag his cloak towards his humble dwelling, each step bringing the woman nearer to safety. The effort was costing him much energy...too much for his advanced age, but finally she was safe inside. He hurried to find cloths with which to bind her injuries and water from his well to clean her wounds. He could see the livid bruises on her face and forehead, the indent of a heavy weapon marking her skin. She was unconscious, and he listened anxiously to her ragged breathing as he bathed her shoulder which had been hacked savagely.

The images swam back before him, shadows of evil emerging from the forest, masked and naked, dragging a blood bespattered body behind them. He had remained frozen with fear in the hide he had fashioned for himself to watch the forest birds. Screaming at the sky, the men hacked at the body with vicious weapons, stamping their feet on the ground as they circled the victim. Laughter, cruel and shrill echoed through the once peaceful clearing as they retreated, leaving behind a bloody mess of shattered bones, pools of blood and hideous murder.

Brother John breathed deeply and opened his eyes to gaze at the light streaming through the unglassed window of the ruined cell. He could hear bird song and smell the wet earth of the surrounding fields, so unlike the stench of blood in that forest clearing. He tried again to focus his mind...

"Out of the depths have I cried to thee, O Lord.."

He could still see the carnage which he had tried to bless before leaving the hide....absolution? The sight was unrecognizable as a man ...but he had tried, before turning away to vomit repeatedly.

It was then that he noticed the woman, lying in the undergrowth, bleeding from gashes in her shoulder and lying as if dead. Shaking with fear he approached and understood that he must get her away from this place lest the masked men returned. Surprisingly they seemed to have forgotten this other victim. His trembling hands grasped her torn undershift, all that was left of her garments, and tugging as gently as he could, he untangled her from the dense undergrowth into which she had fallen. Despite the amount of blood, he somehow managed to lift her onto one of his shoulders, and bent nearly double, he staggered towards his own dwelling near the ruined chapel. She emitted no sound...she was deeply unconscious and her dead weight soon became too much for the frail Brother. Reluctantly he laid her down in the grass and hobbled on towards his home to collect his cloak, hoping this would help him move her for the last bit of the way.

How his old legs had carried him back to the chapel he would never know, but he had managed it by the grace of God, and now fell on his knees to pray for the soul of the unknown victim of such desecration and the still form of the woman, now lying silently in a straw filled paliasse in the corner of his room. He had dressed the dreadful wound in her shoulder and covered her with his cloak, despite the blood stains as it was the warmest thing he possessed and then added the covers from his own bed. He knew she must be kept warm and as he knelt by the paliasse to pray for help, he considered what he should do.

They had come from the direction of the old King's hunting lodge, now little more than a ruin. The forest around was still managed by foresters and verderers but no royal party had used it for many years. Deer, rabbit, boar and birds of all description inhabited the place, normally cool and tranquil. Brother John wondered whether he would ever be able to enjoy that special place again.

Should he seek help for the woman? Could he manage the walk into Gillingham, or maybe into Shaftesbury, climb the hill to the Abbey and seek help from the Abbess? There were few dwellings near his chapel, a ruined place he had found for himself to rest and pray in his old age. The scattered farms and simple homes of the labourers were all mostly clustered round the site of the disused hunting lodge....part of the settlement called Gillingham, but referred to as Motcombe, although certainly growing by the year into a larger place with some comely dwelling places, especially near the church.

How to care for the injured woman was the first priority; he did not feel he could leave her alone at present....he had a smattering of healing knowledge...and he was also afraid of being discovered by the hideously masked men.....devil worshippers....but as soon as she made some little recovery, if that was what the Lord decreed, he would try to walk into the nearest place... possibly the way through Motcombe might be his easiest route now his legs and heart troubled him so. With these decisions restoring his mind somewhat, Brother John sank to his knees in prayer to try and rid himself of the dreadful images which swam through his mind.

Ezekiel Jacobson the barber-surgeon had taken two leisurely days to travel to Shaftesbury to visit his sister and her husband. He was nearing the place now, looking forward to staying with the couple for a few days before returning to his home at Oborne, near Sherborne. The great Abbey stood high on the hill, stretching far into the small town, dominating all with its presence. It was one of the magnificent benefices of the church, tall and solid, and peopled by nuns ordered by their abbess, Margaret Stourton.

The February day was pleasantly warm as he walked his mount gently along the track, admiring the fields of sheep which populated the countryside for miles, for the Abbey had many flocks and was instrumental in the wool trade, bringing much wealth to the Abbey.

He turned off the track when he reached Enmore Green, a small hamlet which, together with the neighbouring hamlet of Motcombe, was really part of the larger, flatter town of Gillingham. He mused on its close proximity to Shaftesbury as he approached his sister's house. Surely it should be part of Shaftesbury, but Gillingham was the larger, more developed place he supposed. His sister's home was at the bottom of the hill, and he was glad of this, as Shaftesbury stood high on a hill, a steep climb, even in the temperate early Spring weather.

The gate, he was surprised to see, was open. Jenna and Isaac were proud of their garden and its environs, and usually kept the gate closed to discourage stray dogs and other animals which might roam freely. He dismounted and rapped on the door with his knuckles, picking up a cloth kerchief caught on a bush by the door and smiling at the anticipation of seeing his sister once more.

There was no answer. Puzzled, he knocked again. The silence deepened, and thinking they may have gone into their rear garden, he stepped round the side of the house, calling her name. The garden was empty, although in one place, there was a trail of broken stems, crushed budding flowers and scuffed earth but no sign of his sister and brother in law.

Knocking once more on the front door, he tried the latch, which to his surprise was open. Inside was a scene of disarray. Chairs had been knocked over, potted herbs upturned, precious books dragged off the wall shelf and scattered on the floor open at random pages, some of which had been trampled..... even vegetables half prepared for a meal, ground into the floor. Ezekiel's knees buckled as he surveyed the room. He guessed with a sinking heart what this meant. He called his sister's name without believing he would receive an answer; he was right; there was silence. He called again, hoping for some response. Nothing. Their one time Jewish faith, despite their family's conversion to Christianity so long ago, had maybe caught up with them in this place they had learned to call home. Ignorance and intolerance seemed to follow them everywhere.

The expulsion of all Jewry from England in 1290 by Edward I had left several Jewish families remaining in England as converted Christians, residing in Domus Conversorum in Chancery Lane, London. There they were able to work, although for very low wages and stay in the country under the protection of priests. Some still secretly observed their Jewish roots. Over the course of a hundred years or more, their life had become less observed, and some families chose to leave, taking their chance in the world as free citizens. Ezekiel's family had been one such, carefully selecting quiet places to set up their homes, and making good use of their many and varied skills to earn a living, but such families were few, and those who had risked everything to remain in a country they had come to regard as home kept themselves to themselves, and lived quietly, thankful of their continuing way of life.

Ezekiel had travelled to the continent to study and to learn how to practice medicine but had returned to England several years ago, alarmed by the persecution now spreading in Italy, where he had a small following of clients grateful for his medical knowledge obtained during some years spent in Greece. He had settled with his wife and two young children near his sister and her husband and was part of the community, although regarded with a certain amount of suspicion by some, despite his family's historic conversion. They were not marked out or openly talked about as Jewish but there was a certain look to the family, a quiet withdrawal from any kind of community activity. As a family, they still observed some Jewish traditions privately, but there was no secret synagogue for them....they celebrated mass with other villagers, as did his sister and her husband. If this made them feel guilty for deserting their ancient Jewish faith, they took care not to show it.

Wearily Ezekiel made an effort to straighten the room so that when he found his sister and brother in law, they would not have to re live their ordeal, and putting his hat on again, he went out to look for them in the town.

To his dismay, he did not find them. Not only that, the small town perched high on the hill was busy as usual and everything seemed in good order. Shaftesbury was a hill town commanding views of the countryside around for miles. It boasted several inns and lesser ale houses, for the Abbey attracted pilgrims come to pray at the shrine of Edward King and Martyr and there was always need for hospitality. There were several markets abounding in the town, which led to traders from villages around as well as further afield coming to trade here. The Abbey itself was wealthy and dominated the town, providing employment for many. There was a market in progress on the cobbled hill just outside the buttressed wall of the Abbey, and Ezekiel recognized neighbours of Jenna and Isaac who expressed surprise that they were not at the market. They had spoken of Ezekiel's intended visit and had meant to purchase hot pies for their meal.

He returned to the house. Isaac's horse was still in the stable and the sleeping chambers were neat and orderly, one laid out ready for himself. What should he do? He searched the house and their little garden for any signs of disturbance, but apart from the upheaval in the kitchen, and the little trail of broken vegetation there was no further indication of where they might be or what might have happened to them. That seemed very strange to him.

Ezekiel was perplexed and troubled. He wandered out of the house hoping to meet neighbours who might have seen them earlier in the day. He called on a couple whom he knew were friends of Jenna. They confirmed that Jenna and Isaac had been at Mass the previous Sunday, and had seemed well, looking forward to his visit but mentioned that they had not seen them since then. This was unusual, as Jenna would normally have visited the market on Monday...and it was now Wednesday.

Ezekiel mounted his horse and moved off in the direction of the guildhall, hoping to find the local bailiff. It was so out of character for his sister to disappear, and why was their room in such disorder? The bailiff knew Jenna and Isaac. They had lived in this small town for a number of years, but he could throw no light on this mysterious absence, in fact, he seemed anxious to be rid of the problem, suggesting that Jenna and Isaac had forgotten his visit, and that an animal of some kind had invaded their kitchen through an open door or window. Ezekiel made extensive enquiries from the surrounding dwellings, but he drew no information. People were friendly and concerned...there was no hint of prejudice or antagonism. Their conversion to

Christianity had taken place many decades ago, an historic family decision. Maybe Ezekiel had come to the wrong conclusion? After all, there had been a very small Jewish community in this town many years ago, and there had been no trouble then.

Several friends gathered over the next few hours, suddenly sharing Ezekiel's unease. They searched the outlying fields, copses and meadows, entered broken down buildings, spoke to tinkers, chapmen, masons.... but Jenna and Isaac appeared to have vanished without trace.

Brother John took his staff and put his sketching parchment in his scrip. It was two days now since the hideous happenings in the forest, and there had been no sound of any disturbance. His patient had not regained consciousness, but the bleeding had stopped, her breathing steadied. He sensed some sort of recovery was a question of time and patience so he was prepared to wait until she was awake before leaving her for long but he needed to return to the glade to banish the memory from his mind. Sometimes when he closed his eyes he could still see the ugly scene. He wanted to return to his hide and watch for the birds, hear their song, glimpse a young deer. This he was confident he could do while the young woman slept.

As he approached the site, his legs shook and beads of sweat trickled down his forehead. His hands felt clammy and damp, and he grasped the stout stick he always carried to help him through the brushwood.

With relief he reached the simple hide he had built, and pushed aside the curtain of ivy and woven twigs. He sank down on the ground, shaking with emotion and fear.

He tried to pray but no words would come at first.... his mind had produced nothing but a blank space. Eventually he felt calmer, and found himself murmuring the words of Thomas a Kempis, "Write thy words O Lord upon my heart..."

He leant back against the bole of the tree which supported his hide and breathed deeply, trying to absorb the peace and hear his beloved birds. He listened in the silence. There was nothing. No bird song, no movement of wild life...just silence.

Hr waited, willing himself to believe that he had simply chosen a strange and unusual moment of quiet, but no birds sang here now, no butterflies danced, no lazy hum of insects.

Clumsily he rose to his feet and grasped his staff. His scrip with his drawing instruments inside would not be used here today. Cautiously he stepped out into the glade. There was very little to be seen of the desecration he had witnessed, but he stumbled nearer to where the fire had been, now just a dead pile of fragmented ash.

With his stick he poked the ashes with care and lifted two or three scorched fragments of cloth from the pile. He felt a duty of care towards this unknown victim; somewhere he must have people who knew who he was. He must find them, but first he must allow the woman to heal.

Ezekiel Jacobson remained in his sister's house for a further week. Jenna's friends and neighbours helped him to right the destroyed kitchen, and together they tended the garden, fed the chickens, continued the search for any clues as to what had befallen Jenna and Isaac, and spread the news both to fellow townspeople as well as the local bailiff and mayor, for Shaftesbury had its own system of authority, closely aligned to the Abbey. Ezekiel was careful in his searching to be discreet in his conversations with people; he had no wish to cast accusations against any local factions, but he was dismayed at the apparent lack of compassionate concern showed by the local bailiff. Finally, aware that his wife would have been expecting him home after just a couple of days, he made arrangements for Isaac's horse to be stabled with the neighbour, locked the house and sick at heart and sorely troubled, he left Shaftesbury.

The track was dry today although there were rain clouds threatening, and Ezekiel made good progress for his horse was freshly rested. He lived in Oborne, very near to the church of St. Cuthbert, a small vill just outside Sherborne.

He had no fear of the track, - he had travelled it many times and knew exactly how long his journey should take him. He had gone some three miles when he heard the thunder of hoof beats behind him. A posse from the bailiff of Shaftesbury cantered round the corner, and skidded to a halt before him.

"Master Jacobson...we have been sent to halt you... Bailiff asks that you return with us."

Ezekiel turned his horse and prepared to accompany the messengers back the way he had come.

Sherborne 1438

Martha Jacobson was anxiously looking forward to the return of her husband. He had not expected to be away so long, and it was time he was home. He was still caring for the young man staying with Master Barton in Milborne Port, and he was due to visit the patient to oversee the fitting of a prosthetic limb which he had fashioned for himself. The patient, Martin Cooper, had been cut to the bone by an assailant in November last, and as he was an amputee, he needed much care in the recovery. Martha understood that he was now doing well and had shown considerable skill with making himself a limb of sorts. It now needed care in attaching and Master Jacobson, with his patience and expertise, was looking forward to this tentative experiment. Martin would need to be patient himself, and only wear the limb for a limited time to start with.

Martha felt restless; it was unlike Ezekiel to stay so long with Jenna and Isaac.

Perhaps she should send the boys to Milborne Port to explain his absence to Master Barton, in whose home Martin Cooper was still lodged. Yes, she would do that tomorrow then there would be no unpleasantness if Ezekiel was truly delayed. Maybe he had fallen unwell. She did not allow her mind to dwell on any other possibility.

The boys walked to Milborne Port from their pleasant home in Oborne, and arrived as Matthias Barton released his scholars for their short midday break. Matthias had not met Ezekiel Jacobson's sons before this, but he recognized them, being so like their father.

"We were expecting your father any day soon," he told them. He thought they looked rather longingly at the boys playing a basic ball game with a pig's bladder in the field.

"Our mother sent us to tell you that he seems to be delayed in Shaftesbury. We were expecting him home several days ago, but he is with his sister, my aunt Jenna, and he has not yet returned. She said to tell you that he will call on you as soon as he returns."

"Martin will be disappointed," remarked Matthias, "he has been counting the days so that he can try out his new leg."

The younger boy looked puzzled, and Matthias explained that Martin had been severely wounded in the fighting in France, and had lost the lower part of one leg. He had now carved a false limb which Master Jacobson had agreed to help him with. The boys watched the game in the field whilst they drank cold water from the well. Matthias offered to allow them to join in the game, but they shrank back with a polite nod of thanks, and started off for home.

"I hope Master Jacobson will be home soon," Martin said, when he heard of the delay. He had made several attempts at the false limb, each one being slightly different. Davy, Matthias' serving man, had fetched him suitable wood whenever he had seen it, and the barn where Martin made his home for the moment was littered with shavings and polished or half completed limbs.

But Master Jacobson did not appear that week, and everyone in the household was disappointed for Martin's delay.

"Maybe I should ride over and see Mistress Jacobson," Matthias suggested, when the week stretched yawningly on.

He rode over the following morning, leaving his scholars in Martin's care for an hour or two. He arrived to find the home in a state of distress. One of the bailiff's men from Shaftesbury was in the house with Mistress Jacobson remonstrating with her, whilst the boys stood with their maid servant in the hall listening in terrified silence.

Matthias gathered that some harm had befallen Jenna and Isaac, and the bailiff had arrested Ezekiel for their murder, despite no evidence of bodies.

"What is it you wish Mistress Jacobson to do?" Matthias asked, interrupting the tirade. The man looked at Matthias suspiciously.

"Who are you?" he asked, ill natured to the core.

"Matthias Barton, friend of the Jacobsons. How can I help?" The man laughed derisively.

"I need to take Mistress Jacobson with me to Shaftesbury. She may be required to answer some pertinent questions."

"I'm sure that can be arranged. Let me consult the Coroner, and you will find there will be no problem."

"The Coroner?" the man said, clearly taken aback.

"The Coroner of Dorset and Master Jacobson are old friends who are working together on one particular problem."

The man was dumbfounded, and Matthias' heart was beating so hard that he was surprised it didn't show. How could he have dared speak for the Coroner in such a way? He didn't even know whether he was at home. However, Matthias and the Coroner were old friends and Matthias hoped he would not let him down. He felt in his gut that something was not right here.

Sir Tobias Delaware, Coroner of Dorset, was at home, but it was late afternoon before he arrived at the house of the Jacobsons, and the bailiff's man was becoming surly and impatient. When he met the Coroner his manner changed somewhat and he tried hard to ingratiate himself with Sir Tobias, who was not deceived.

"We will ride together in the morning," Sir Tobias told the man. "I will come myself, but Mistress Jacobson will remain here with her sons. Master Jacobson needs to return here, and I will vouchsafe his remaining in this house." His tone brooked no argument, and however much the man protested, it fell on deaf ears. He was sent away to find lodgings for the night in nearby Sherborne.

Shaftesbury.

Ezekiel Jacobson was living in a nightmare; he had returned with the posse as a free man, concerned about the reason for his return and since arriving in Shaftesbury had been arrested for the suspected murder of his sister and brother in law. His continued enforced stay in the small castle was uncomfortable and undignified, but he had no-one to speak for him; furthermore, he was overcome with grief at the possible fate of his sister and her husband.....he could not take in the fact that he might never see her neat figure throwing open her front door with her wide welcoming smile and he was further dismayed to learn that his wife had been summoned to speak against him.

The discoloured walls of the holding cell where he had been detained were thick and damp. He had been held here for three days now, and his garments were stained and filthy. Normally an impeccably dressed man, Ezekiel was shamed by his unshaven state, his sweat stained clothes and his need to use a corner of the cell for his bodily needs. The cell was rat infested and dark, the only light coming from a small unglassed window, too high for him to be able to see outside. At least he had not been fettered.

He heard the approach of his jailor, heavy footsteps scuffing up the narrow stone steps. A jangle of keys, and the door swung open. He was pushed unceremoniously to his feet and jabbed in the back to impel him to stumble out of the cell and down the stone steps. No word had been spoken directly to him, but he was aware of resentful muttering from the jailor.

He found Sir Tobias waiting in the ante room of the castle, thunderous and testy.

"There has been no evidence of bodies and yet you have detained this man? On what grounds? Master Jacobson – Good day to you. I will have my say with these bunglers before we leave for home. Your wife is most concerned." The bailiff began to protest.

"This man was riding away from Shaftesbury because he knew what had happened to his relatives but he will not tell us. He had no need to linger further. He had done the deed." As his accusations continued his voice rose in a shrill squeak. Sir Tobias found himself wondering whether the man had all his wits about him.

"What you are telling me has no logic whatsoever," he said, sharply. "Master Jacobson had travelled from Oborne that very morning….how could he have been in two places at once?"

"We are a law abiding community here," the bailiff began, "we do not allow felons to escape... we have our own mayor, we have the presence of the Abbey, we have…"

"….and you have a somewhat foolish bailiff," finished Sir Tobias, acidly. "Master Jacobson should not have been arrested. His sister and brother in law may have been the victims of an unseemly murder, or they may simply have gone away without telling neighbours, unlikely as that sounds."

Master Jacobson had been reunited with his horse and permitted to wash, although somewhat sketchily, so without further delay they left Shaftesbury and began the sombre ride home.

The journey home to Milborne Port and Oborne was uneventful. Ezekiel Jacobson was silent, withdrawn, and Sir Tobias allowed him to be so. Ezekiel insisted that he be permitted to continue to Oborne alone. Purse Caundle, where the Coroner lived, was the first destination reached and so the Coroner agreed. He felt instinctively that Master Jacobson was not guilty of any crime, and would willingly travel back with him to Shaftesbury or Gillingham if so required.

Sherborne

Martha Jacobson was relieved to see her husband, but he would give no details in front of their two young sons. She was perturbed to see his pallor, his eyes reddened from weeping and the dishevelled state of his person. He changed his clothes on arrival, washed his face and hands in the perfumed warm water Martha heated for him and toyed with the food she set before him.

When the boys had gone to their sleeping chamber, he told her the story, pausing now and again to choose his words with care. He wanted to cleanse himself of the memory...of the imaginings....but he would not burden her with the full details of the attack on himself. She listened in silence, tears welling in her eyes.

"You will return to Shaftesbury?"

"I need to search for my beautiful sister and her husband so I will. I am fortunate that I have a slight acquaintance with Sir Tobias through my dealings with Martin Cooper, who was so badly injured before Christmas, so I doubt they will arrest me again."

As he travelled to the home of Matthias the next day to see Martin Cooper, he pondered carefully on how best to conduct his search. Although there was urgency about the search, he must see Martin first to start him on his new journey.

Matthias greeted him warmly, aware of the circumstances of his absence, and wishing to show support and friendship. Martin was waiting eagerly for him in the barn, his prosthetic ready for a first trial.

Master Jacobson was grateful for the problem confronting him - it was good to have this task to occupy his mind. He first massaged Martin's stump with an ointment made from periwinkle and musk mallow to relieve any inflammation, and then examined the limb which Martin had chosen. It seemed to him to follow amazingly well the contours of the stump. Just below the top of the limb, Martin had gouged a channel wide enough for thin straps of leather, and onto these were further straps at right angles which would be fastened to a strap which was attached tightly round his remaining thigh. The success of this basic means of support rather relied on how tightly Martin could bear the thigh strap. If it was loose, the limb would be too insecure to be of any use. It took some time to make the first attachment, but Martin had learned to be patient, and Ezekiel Jacobson was a gentle worker.

"Are you able to stand unaided?" he asked Martin, when the first try at the straps was made.

"I'm not certain- help me up and steady me."

Ezekiel took him by both hands and raised him up carefully. He held him for a moment or two while Martin put his weight on his sound leg, now fully knitted after the vicious cuts he had received although visibly scarred. Cautiously Martin tried his weight on the new limb, distributing his weight gradually. At first he thought it would break it felt so unnatural, and when he tried to balance alone, he would have fallen had Ezekiel not caught him and lowered him onto the bench. The second attempt was a little more successful. Martin experimented with his balance, moving carefully from side to side to give his new leg the feel of being there.

"I think that is as far as you should go for the first few days. Try this as an exercise each day...two or three times daily. I will leave the balm with you....you need to massage this into your leg before you attach the limb to avoid friction. It must be comfortable before we try any steps."

Martin regretfully placed the little pot of balm back in Master Jacobson's hand.

"I cannot afford to pay you for this, Sir. I can use grease from the kitchen."

"Accept this as a gift from me. I am anxious to see how we can make this work for you, so allow me to help our experiment along"

Martin flushed slightly, aware of his impoverished state, but grateful for the gesture.

"Thank you for your generosity – and I'm sorry for your trouble."

The barber-surgeon acknowledged Martin's words gravely, and prepared to leave.

"I will call again in three days. Practice putting it on and balancing. We'll try a step or two when I return."

Matthias forestalled him as he came from the barn.

"A word in private, Master Jacobson...step into the schoolroom for a moment."

Matthias was aware that the old religion into which he had been born would be very strong. What he wanted to say must be said in private with no risk to anyone.

"Let me be direct, Master Jacobson. Are there any signs of Jewishness in the house of your sister?"

Ezekiel understood the need to be cautious, even with Matthias.

"Are you accusing my sister and her husband of violating their partaking of the sacrament?"

"Not at all. I have no doubts concerning your family's historic conversion, their attendance at Mass and their belief in the blessed Eucharist. Nor that of yourself and your family. I wanted to ask you in confidence whether you feel there is any evidence of their old faith in the house which might be damaging should it be found by whoever is behind their disappearance.."

Ezekiel sat down weakly and passed his hands over his face wearily.

"I am at a loss as to know. Somewhere in their house will be one or two precious reminders of their birthright and heritage. I should like to find them and remove them for safety but I am nervous about a return to the house. I am not convinced that this disappearance is anything to do with our heritage, but it would be good to be certain."

"Would you accept myself as a companion to return to Shaftesbury to search and retrieve them? It occurs to me that if there is any evidence in the home, it would be better to find and remove it. We could also search the surrounding countryside."

"Why would you offer to do this for me?" Ezekiel Jacobson wondered.

"Perhaps because I have travelled and seen a wider canvas than local men; perhaps because I have experienced personal loss from which I am still recovering; perhaps because I just want to help in this desperately sad situation. You have helped Martin in his need and I cannot even begin to think how I would feel if we had been unable to give my family a fitting memorial."

"I intend to pay for a chantry priest to say daily mass for their souls if they are found deceased, but yes, I would welcome a retrieval of any more personal items."

"Then when would you like to go, Master Jacobson? Your experience has not been a happy one in Shaftesbury; I can understand you not wishing to put yourself at risk."

"Let me discuss this with my wife," Ezekiel decided, "and you will need to make arrangements for your scholars."

Matthias smiled. "While Martin is still here, he is well used to the routine, and Lady Alice enjoys a spell in the schoolroom."

The Coroner was not easy with Matthias travelling alone with Ezekiel; he had a gut feeling about the disappearance of Jenna and Isaac which did not sit well. He decided to travel with them to prevent any further arrest of Ezekiel. He also wanted to revisit the town to question the bailiff again, whose swift arrest of Master Jacobson had given him cause to wonder. Lady Alice and Martin were well briefed by Matthias before they left, the little party setting out for a two day sojourn to Shaftesbury with serious questions running through their minds.

Martin found attaching the limb on his own quite challenging, and Davy quickly became adept at helping him. It needed to be fitted very exactly, the slightest bit out of position would encourage the friction that Master Jacobson had been so anxious to avoid. Once attached, Martin followed the same routine three times daily, rocking gently from side to side, allowing his weight to rest on the new leg.

Lady Alice, the Coroner's daughter, had become an enthusiastic teacher in Matthias' place, and enjoyed times when Matthias was absent, moving among the young scholars, encouraging, repeating lessons, using both Latin and the English tongue. She had been well taught by her father, who was a great believer in good education, rare for women. Alice was grateful for this, and loved her times in Matthias' school room.

However, not all was progressing as Alice would have liked. Widowed under a slight cloud, she was aware that her father was beginning to cast around for a new alliance for her. He had made several journeys to Sherborne recently which were not part of his work as Coroner, and Alice was afraid that he had made contact with families of a similar social standing to make enquiries which may not have been as subtle as Alice would have wished. She was quite happy to remain in the family home with her son Luke...Sir Tobias had persuaded her to stay after the Christmas twelve day feast, and Alice, knowing that she must make some concessions, had agreed. Her maid servant had been taken into the household with her, and the lodge house now remained empty.

Today, Alice was working with the oldest boys who had progressed exceptionally well, and who needed new challenges. Alice wanted to make them speak...to encourage them to think as well as to write and copy. Their copy slates were neat; the formation of letters was accurate; their recitation of scriptures was fluent....now for some logic. Martin worked quietly with the younger, less advanced boys, including Luke, Alice's son. That was a further problem, Alice thought. Luke would move on to the school in Sherborne, run by Thomas Copeland for the monks of the Abbey. He would board, and she would be alone. How would she occupy herself? Her situation was such that she could only expect an older, well placed suitor....she wished for more for herself but that seemed sinfully ungrateful. She had found a kind of peace in the small amount of time she had spent in the schoolroom....a second marriage would deprive her of that pleasure. She wished Matthias was more outgoing and had male friends of his own age that she could converse with – but he had allowed few people into his world, it seemed to Alice.

She remembered the only occasion she had observed emotion from him....when he had suddenly allowed Elizabeth, Davy's wife, to take her to the chest in the solar to find clothes for the child Ennis...clothes which had belonged to his dead sisters. When they returned with the garments, Alice remembered seeing Matthias' eyes filled with tears...but when she glanced at him again, he had brushed them away and was his usual courteous self. She sighed as she gathered the three boys around to start their discussion on a logic problem she had devised for them.....Matthias was an enigma to her – rather cold yet apparently generous to strangers, polite without showing warmth, loyal to Martin through his many troubles and certainly passionate about his fledgling schoolroom. Difficult to break into his thoughts, she felt, which were carefully hidden.....but willing to assist her father with some of his enquiries...like today, for instance...offering to go to Shaftesbury with Master Jacobson to seek some answers.

Whilst Alice bent her mind to guiding the three boys through their discussion, Martin's mind flicked more than once to his growing friendship with Lydia, the young mother of Freya and now the adopted mother of Ennis. He hoped for nothing more than friendship – his chances of anything more were vanished with his injuries, but he found her company peaceful and undemanding. Like himself, Lydia appeared to want nothing more than an easy friendship, and he liked to see her smile when he appeared, hobbling on his crutches, his tools strapped round his waist. He had now made several valuable repairs and improvements to her humble thatched cottage, improved by the Coroner's generous donation when she agreed to take Ennis in. She too was a widow, made so by the murder of her young husband the night before Freya was born. They were both what Matthias had once described as waifs and strays, but Martin now understood him to have spoken in jest. He felt as easy with Matthias as he did with Lydia, and he would miss them if he had to move on. That was another of his problems...he really should move out....he could not impose for ever on the generosity of Matthias. Each with their own private thoughts and problems, Alice and Martin worked well together in the schoolroom.

Shaftesbury

Journeying towards Shaftesbury, the three men discussed how to begin their wider search for Jenna and Isaac, how they might involve their neighbours, who had a wider sense of the immediate locality and whether it was worth requesting help from the somewhat disinterested bailiff.

Ezekiel's thoughts were with his sister and her husband as they drew near to the house. He remembered the happiness he had felt as he had tapped on their door, quite ignorant of the horror he was to face. The house was as he left it; he was relieved at that. He had wondered if the perpetrators would return and ransack the house, but there was no sign of a break-in of any kind.

Sir Tobias and Matthias searched the house with Ezekiel, but nothing untoward was found. The Coroner sat alone in the pleasant garden waiting for Ezekiel to complete his final task, lost in his own thoughts. He had visited the manor of Poyntington recently with a view to seeking an alliance for Lady Alice, but he was uncertain of the wisdom of such a move. Matthias meanwhile prowled round the garden, searching for any signs of disturbance, but there was nothing further to be seen.

"They tried to leave some signs of their enforced removal," Matthias said. Sir Tobias rubbed his hands across his face.

"I had not thought so far, but no, they did not leave willingly. Did Isaac drop the kerchief deliberately? Did they try to resist?"

Matthias was silent. He was aware from private conversation with him that Ezekiel Jacobson's family had converted to Christianity many decades ago and had been part of the conversion house in London. Ezekiel would not even have been born at that time but old traditions of faith die hard through such generations. He now lived a quiet life, working as the local barber-surgeon when so required. He had saved Martin Cooper's life by his skill and dedication, and earned the respect of all who had been involved in that frightening episode.

"We must see the bailiff in Shaftesbury as soon as Ezekiel has finished here. I want to know why he was arrested so suddenly. There is still no evidence of bodies."

Ezekiel joined them shortly after this. He was carrying a small bundle which he strapped on to his saddle carefully before they left, latching the door securely behind him. He called on the neighbour who had stabled the horse and had conversation with him before trotting after the Coroner and Matthias.

The bailiff was displeased to see them. They were met with a barely concealed scowl. "I have no news for you," he began, brusquely, "except that this man should be in custody." He indicated Ezekiel as he spoke.

"I think not, bailiff. We have no bodies....and Master Jacobson was at home in Oborne until he arrived at his sister's home to find her missing." The bailiff grunted.

"What caused you to arrest this man?" Sir Tobias asked him.

"I believe he was instrumental in this disappearance, which surely resulted in death."

"How did you reach that conclusion?" Sir Tobias asked, coldly. He was unimpressed by this bailiff, who faltered under the stern eyes of the Coroner. He had no reasonable answer to his question, but he blundered on.

"The man was suspect in our community. The brother was protecting his own very being..."

"Nonsense!" exploded Matthias, who had listened with increasing anger.

"Jenna and Isaac had lived in Shaftesbury for years... they heard mass regularly, took the Eucharist on Holy days and lived God fearing Christian lives. Master Jacobson had visited them many times before. What are you saying, man?"

"I live in this community. You do not," snarled the bailiff. "I hear things which give me cause to suspect unnatural practices..."

"Such as?" Matthias demanded, hotly. Sir Tobias laid a calming hand on Matthias' shoulder. "Describe these practices, bailiff," he ordered.

"I cannot bring myself to utter them."

"Then they are a figment of your imagination."

A disturbance in the street outside the hall where they had met the bailiff came nearer and nearer...there was shouting, cries of distress, running feet and as the door burst open unceremoniously, a welter of humanity crowded round the door, pushing a forester before them.

"Horrific things I've seen in the deer pale...near the forest...my lords...come and see..."

The bailiff pushed his way to the door and roughly shoved the crowd out onto the street, grasping the forester by the arm and leading him further into the room. He stood sweating and shaking, his eyes wild.

He described how he had gone into the deer pale to repair fences, then moving deeper into the surrounding forest to set traps had chanced across two men dancing wildly round the remains of a fire. He approached them and was suddenly terrified by their ghastly masked appearance, horned masks with dripping red mouths and bulbous eyes, like the devil himself. They advanced on him as if to attack, but as he raised his stave to strike them they laughed maniacally and leapt over him, disappearing into the forest at speed. He approached the fire, and to his horror, he discovered the burnt and disfigured remains of a woman, bloodstains surrounding the place of the fire.

"The woman was dead, my lords...cut and disfigured...."

"Lead us to the place!" the bailiff commanded. He glared at the Coroner, as if daring him to counteract his command, but Sir Tobias merely nodded and followed, Matthias and Ezekiel Jacobson close behind.

The forester led them past the Abbey and followed the pathway towards the settlement of Motcombe, once the sight of King John's hunting lodge. They skirted Enmore Green, descended into Motcombe, passed Latchmere Pond and when level with Coppleridge they followed Cusborne Lake and entered the thickest part of the deer park, stumbling onwards towards the great deer pale. They led their horses most of the way as the forester had arrived by foot, and arrived at the place, near to a sudden open space surrounded by clumps of heavier, thicker trees. The fire was now extinguished although still warm. The disfigured body of a young woman was crumpled in the ashes, her throat discoloured by the garrotte ligament tightly embedded in the flesh.

Sir Tobias knelt on the ground by the fire, heedless of the mud and ash. The ground was still faintly warm. The bailiff hung back behind Matthias. Ezekiel closed his eyes and withdrew, fearing to look.

The Coroner turned the girl gently towards him, revealing the frozen rictus grin of horror on her dead face. Her tongue protruded from her mouth, blue from asphyxiation; her staring eyes bulged in their sockets; a deep slash from her collar bone to the waist, slicing through her once white linen undergarments revealed that the purpose had been to slice into her body. What was left of her clothes and the ground around her was soaked in blood.

"Devil worshippers," the bailiff whispered, hoarse with fear. He glared at Ezekiel.

Matthias glanced at him. He was white to the lips, shaking all over. Matthias put a hand on his shoulder to calm him.

"Sit, sir. You will fall down else."

The bailiff sank down on a fallen log nearby and put his head in his hands.

Sir Tobias straightened up. "If the forester had not disturbed them, they would have cut her to ribbons. Her remains would have been burned on the fire. What monstrosity are we dealing with here?"

He looked again at the girl. Where it was visible, the flesh was white and smooth contrasting more vividly with the blood, now congealing in pools around her. Her feet were bare, but her toes were scraped and muddy, the toe nails cruelly splintered and broken, indicating that she had been dragged some way. Her head was almost bald, the hair no more than tiny spikes.

"We must remove her to the death house." Sir Tobias looked at the bailiff, aware that he was in danger of treading on the toes of the authority of Shaftesbury, but the bailiff was in no state to issue commands or take decisions. He sat where Matthias had guided him, half fainting.

The forester was made of stronger stuff; he fetched a wooden hurdle from nearby and assisted by the Coroner and Matthias, they placed the poor body on the hurdle and with the forester and Ezekiel's assistance made a sad procession back the way they had come, the bailiff bringing up the rear, leading his own and Ezekiel's mounts.

By the time they reached Shaftesbury the bailiff had recovered somewhat and directed them to the death house of Trinity church. His colour had returned and so had his bombastic manner.

"Thank you for your assistance, Sir Tobias. I will call upon our own coroner now to assist me." Despite his apparent assured confidence there was an underlying nervousness which caused him to flick his eyes from side to side as if seeking something undecipherable. Matthias watched him closely.

Sir Tobias was minded to protest that their own coroner had not observed the situation and then changed his mind. He needed to tread carefully; Shaftesbury was a borough in its own right and had an appointed hierarchy of officials, all within the watchful brief of the Abbey here. He would observe carefully to see how this bailiff managed the case. Shaftesbury was well endowed with lawgivers and did have a coroner of its own as well as the bailiff and a mayor, not to mention twelve churches and the wealthy abbey with its huge influx of pilgrims. They even had two representatives in parliament, although rarely seen locally. He had come not to act in his official capacity but to support Ezekiel Jacobson and to ensure that he was not re-arrested. Let that be his role for now.

Feeling there was little else they could add to the new death in Shaftesbury, Matthias and Ezekiel suggested they should begin their journey home. Sir Tobias was not so enthusiastic about leaving so soon, desirous of observing how the matter was dealt with. He also wished to know the identity of the corpse. The coroner had not appeared although messengers had been dispatched to his dwelling at Cann, and there was a depressing air of listlessness about the case.

The bailiff explained haltingly that he could not identify the girl. She was not a known inhabitant of the town, and thus should be interred in the grave plots with all due speed. Sir Tobias could not help but disagree.

"You have not enquired of the townspeople whether any knew her," he objected.

"My deputy and I know all the inhabitants of the town. She is not known to us. She must be a vagrant," the bailiff declared.

"Not good enough, my man," replied Sir Tobias. "Look at her flesh...soft, smooth. Did you not observe her feet? She had clearly worn soft shoes to protect her feet, which were damaged by the rough ground over which she had been dragged."

"I was too distressed to notice such details, my lord Coroner."

"Where is your own borough coroner? He should be here by now."

"We have sent for him; he enjoys his drink too early in the day sometimes.."

"We should not have to wait for him. With your permission I will begin the examination of the corpse myself in his absence."

The Coroner strode out of the bailiff's rooms and crossed the square, passing down Bimport where the way led to Trinity Church, close to the gatehouse of the Abbey, into whose death house the girl had been taken. Matthias and Ezekiel followed uneasily. The bailiff and his deputy were forced to half run to keep pace with the Coroner who reached the death house before them and pushed the door open. Inside it was cool and dark. The stench of death was strong, partially disguised by bowls of herbs set to burn in bowls set around the walls. An elderly priest was arranging the body decorously and humming a tuneless dirge as he worked.

Sir Tobias approached the stone slab on which the young woman had been placed. The priest looked alarmed, and moved to protect her, but Sir Tobias spoke softly to him, assuring him of his office and his intention to examine the body with care and respect.

"Matthias, mark well my findings. I have no scribe today and I would not wish to forget my comments at a later date should we need further information."

Matthias stepped nearer and willed himself to concentrate as Sir Tobias began his examination.

The Coroner took note of the garrotte cord – a thin leather cord wickedly embedded in the soft flesh and the viciously accurate slash across the chest, which would have exposed rib cage and heart had the forester not disturbed the ritual. There were broken fingers on one hand where the girl had fought back, the bloodied feet with crushed toe nails, the grazed knees indicating more dragging of the captured victim and the bruised face, disfiguring further what was once a pretty young woman. He paused, noting that Ezekiel had left the death house, unable to bear this catalogue of injuries, aware that this same fate might have been meted out to his sister and her husband. He continued, examining the costly fine undergarment worn but now torn – a shift of soft fabric unadorned with any embroidery or other marking. He noted the hair on the head, deliberately shorn so close to the head that it was impossible to determine the colour of the hair. There were burn marks on one leg, close to the heel and extending up the calf where her captors had held her close to the fire.

"Sweet Mary!" exclaimed Matthias, breathing deeply and aware that he was sweating freely. "Is this what may have been done to Jenna and Isaac?"

The Coroner nodded, folding his arms as he completed his examination. The bailiff stood some way off, watching closely.

"Are you finished, Sir Tobias?" he called.

The Coroner was about to reply when the door to the death house crashed open and a lean individual in a long black robe open at the front revealing a stained jerkin tucked into dark green hose stood panting in the opening. The light behind him from outside made it hard to see his face. The soft buskins on his feet were impractical for outdoor use and told of confused and hurried dressing.

"I have come to examine the corpse," he slurred, steadying himself on the door latch as he swayed on his feet.

"You are too late, Daniel," scowled the bailiff, sourly.

"I am the coroner...it is my task to do this.." the Shaftesbury coroner walked unsteadily towards Sir Tobias, eyeing him with hostility born of drink.

"Who are you? By what authority have you usurped my position?"

"I suggest you return to your home and sleep off the effects of your over-indulgence, my friend. I am the Coroner for Dorset, empowered by the Sheriff of Dorset who holds his office from His Grace the King himself. Do you wish to discuss this further? I have made a proper examination of the unfortunate girl in the appropriate manner. I will have my scribe deliver you a transcript of my findings. Now go home."

"You are too late, Daniel" repeated the bailiff, heavily.

His deputy took Daniel by the arm and ushered him away, muttering words to him which Matthias was unable to hear. The bailiff looked uncomfortable.

"I thank you for your forbearance of our coroner's weakness," he said. "Is this now complete? We need to bury the young woman now."

"Not until this death has been made public in the town, bailiff. You say you know everyone, but someone must know her or have seen her. We should know who she is if possible before burial. Master Jacobson had absolutely nothing to do with this – or the disappearance of his relatives. I still find it incomprehensible that you should have arrested him with no evidence and no visible bodies."

The bailiff had the good sense to look suitably crushed by the Coroner's words as they left the death house to join Ezekiel outside.

"Let me see you organize an inquiry into this episode," commanded Sir Tobias to the bailiff. "Is your local coroner often thus?"

"Not often, my lord," was the reply, but he did not meet Sir Tobias' eyes as he said it.

They left the bailiff to start his enquiries, although Sir Tobias expressed doubts as to whether it would be done with enthusiastic vigour. He did not feel he could press the issue much more, being so far away and with Shaftesbury having its own system of authority.

They walked slowly through the market place, shaken by the extent of the visible injuries inflicted and the lack of vigorous leadership.

"This really does shriek of evil practices," Sir Tobias muttered, "and I am suspicious of the manner in which the bailiff will pursue the identity of the victim. I am concerned about the appearance of their coroner, - if he was under the influence of drink, I did not smell it on him, yet he was clearly not himself."

"So what do you propose to do?" Matthias asked, dodging a small boy staggering across the market place under the weight of buckets of water.

"There is little we can do at present. I will return in a day or two to observe how matters have progressed for the sake of Ezekiel, but meanwhile, we have no choice but to return home."

Sir Tobias was thoughtful as they prepared to leave the town. The Abbey of Shaftesbury was rich indeed and its presence dominated this hill top place. It was a town of many churches and the mayor and other persons of authority appeared to have risen as high as the Abbess in authority, but he sensed an unseemly abuse of power with which he felt uncomfortable. He was the Coroner for Dorset, and Shaftesbury was within the county, but it was also a borough in its own right and had appointed its own borough officers who must be permitted to fulfil their duties.

As he watched them retrieve their horses, the bailiff of Shaftesbury determined to bury the girl without further delay.

Sherborne

Meanwhile fifteen miles distant, Sherborne was far from peaceful. Abbot Bradford could not allow the towns-people to forget their debt to him after the fire in the Abbey, and his bailiff was in constant communication with tithing men in the hundreds to remind them that payment for the damage must be made. There were minor scuffles, hard words exchanged and sullen atten-dance at Mass, which for most people was obligatory. Walter Gallor, who had smashed the illegal font, was back in his shop and was very vociferous concerning the incident. He blamed the Earl of Huntingdon's men for their involvement, which had stirred up the riot leading to the fire and resolutely refused to accept any blame himself for his actions. There was a faction of folk who refused to use his shop and turned their trade to other fleshers in the Shambles. Resentment still smouldered but conversely, there was also a movement afoot to raise funds for the new almshouse, and hand in hand with the unease and fury over the Abbot's debt was a generous spirit of giving towards the almshouse.

There had been a small house of mercy in the town for some years, but there was now a feeling that a more generous one should be built on the piece of ground close to the Abbey, adding to the existing plot. Margaret Gough was already applying her social connections avidly to raising funds and materials for the project, and His Grace the King was being petitioned by Bishop Neville of Salisbury to grant a licence for the new and improved almshouse. Indeed, many expenses had already been incurred by one William Keylewey in procuring this licence from the King. Richard Rochell accompanied him and was the chief organizer in their journeying, and his careful planning was invaluable. Dame Margaret Gough was behind them, and Richard Rochell painstakingly kept meticulous accounts. For the accounts were very important, as they all knew. Abbot Bradford was insistent that recompense should be made for his damaged Abbey, and Richard Rochell was at pains to keep the two accounts separate.

It was indeed strange that with such unrest and ill feeling in the small town, people should at the same time be so generous to the great project of the building. Their taxes to the Abbot were one thing – but the building of the Almshouse was their own project. Abbot Bradford played no part in this – would probably not even contribute to it as Richard Rochell bitterly commented as he wrote up his accounts, but once His Grace King Henry had bestowed his licence on them, they would be utterly free of the influence of the Abbot – in this, at least.

As he entered items in his accounts, he reflected on the history of the house of mercy. He paused as he thought back over the years. He had been involved in the scheme for many years, since 1419 when he had been a church warden; he remembered the day he, John Searle and William Wygrim had made a covenant bringing the old house of mercy into existence. It was inscribed on parchment and indented into three parts, and locked for safe keeping into the chest in which he kept all these precious accounts.

How very different from Abbot Bradford's demands for money...and yet somehow the hard pressed people of Sherborne managed to rise to the occasion with willing hearts. They had no choice as far as Abbot Bradford's demands were concerned....the market was taxed, the ale was taxed, the mills charged high prices – they belonged to the Abbot...even their festivities were taxed.

"Time to put it all behind you, Richard," declared Margaret Gough, as she regarded him in the light of the candles. She knew him well – he would be full of regrets for the distressing conflict with the Abbot.... full of what might have been had things been different – better, she thought, to dwell on what they had achieved...

"Tomorrow I plan to go to each tithing to ask for donations, however small. We are working on obtaining the licence – now we must consider the cost of building."

Richard put his accounts away, glancing across at Dame Gough. She was a handsome woman of middle years, widowed and wealthy. She had a strong social conscience, and had supported the building of the rogue font in All Hallows, as had Richard. They were part of the leading group of townspeople who opposed the Abbot and kept themselves very much up to date regarding town affairs.

"I shall start with our good friend the Coroner," Dame Margaret decided. "Then there are priests of the town and gentlefolk in surrounding villages as well as the tithings within the town. We'll meet again when I have completed the collection."

"God be praised for Sherborne! Despite the ill natured feeling towards the Abbot, we have a generous spirit abounding in our town."

"That is so, but the Abbot has caused less wealthy people to be hard pressed. To pay for his building repairs, he has raised so many taxes that there is little pleasure for many, - and yet by virtue of the King's licence, people are still willing to give whatever they can for the building of the almshouse. It seems a symbol of our freedom from the Abbot."

Dame Margaret's assessment of the situation was a wisely considered one, and on this note of optimism, they went their separate ways.

Several days later Richard Rochell of Sherborne was planning the next visit to London with William Keylewey. Dame Margaret was hosting their meeting. A good brew of ale and a roaring fire in her comfortable home promised a profitable evening of preparation. Richard had already procured the services of a scrivener to inscribe the necessary documents when the time came, and they waited for William to arrive to prepare for their next visit, which would be longer, and therefore more costly.

He was late, unusual for him, and seemed out of sorts, pale in countenance and flustered.

"Dame Margaret, you must excuse me," he said, after short while, "I am not myself this evening. We have had a sharp shock which has quite taken the energy from me."

He swirled his ale in its cup, watching the pattern of the pale golden liquid.

"My daughter has returned from Shaftesbury. I know not how to deal with this."

The assembled company of friends were silent. William and Sarah's daughter had been placed in the great nunnery at Shaftesbury, for William Keylewey was a man of some substance financially and had observed his daughter's lack of dignity, simple mind and wandering eyes with young men. He had paid good silver for her admittance, and he and his wife were convinced that the novitiate would tame and calm her wayward character and ease her disordered mind.

"She is tired and dirty...her gown is torn and she tells a wild tale about masked men. My daughter was ever one for fancy tales that lack the truth...and I fear I must return her to the Abbey. If I do not, the Mistress of novices will send for her."

"Did she travel alone?" Dame Margaret asked, concerned by the story.

"Apparently she left with a companion after they were both reprimanded for inability to obey the silence."

"Where is her companion now? Are they both in your house?"

"She lost sight of her companion it seems when she took a lift with a cloth trader who had a cart."

"Perhaps the companion had the good sense to return to the Abbey before it was too late," Richard Rochell commented. William Keylewey nodded sadly. His daughter was a sore trial to them, and he knew he would have to return his wayward daughter to the Abbess, at least for the moment. If she was proving too difficult, perhaps he would be asked to remove her altogether. He began to speak about the items needed for their forthcoming journey , but it was without his usual vigour, and after a short while, he excused himself to return to his home.

Margaret Goffe was a woman of her word. Despite the cold wind which blew through the streets of Sherborne coming in from the distant coast and bearing rain on its back, she tracked Sir Tobias down several days later with her ledger of promises of donations towards the almshouses.

"What may I put against your name?" she enquired, unwilling to beat about the bush. May as well be straightforward with such a task, and she knew Sir Tobias was a plain speaking man.

"I had thought to offer three days labour from two of my best men," he suggested.

"Anything else?" Dame Goffe gave her best smile to Sir Tobias, and he was won over, offering more than he intended, but glad to do so.

"I understand the arrangements for the licence are well on the way Dame Goffe? Is it Master Keylewey who is undertaking the travel and adventure?"

"Indeed it is, together with Master Rochell," agreed the widow, "although sadly Master Keylewey has a mite of trouble at home. His daughter has absconded from her position in Shaftesbury Abbey, scrambled home somehow with tales of masked men on the track and so far is refusing to return."

"Is this the daughter who tells tale tales of strange events to anyone who will listen to her nonsense?"

"The same, Sir Tobias."

"But she talks of masked men....this is one story I'd like to hear."

Sarah Keylewey was at home with her daughter, locked in fierce argument as Sir Tobias approached the house. He knocked hard to allow them time to subdue their quarrel, and waited for an answer. It came after a short pause, the door opened by a small, frightened looking maidservant.

"May I speak with your mistress?"

"Please to enter, Sir....my mistress will be down in a moment."

Sarah Keylewy had obviously taken the opportunity to leave the room and compose herself. She appeared directly, bobbing a curtsy to Sir Tobias.

"My husband is out at present, Sir," she began. Sir Tobias stopped her, holding up his hand.

"No, it is your daughter I would like to speak to, with your permission."

"Have they sent you to take her back to Shaftesbury?"

"Not at all. I am nothing to do with Shaftesbury or the Abbey. Why do you say so?"

"The Abbess has a reputation for sending her bailiff after girls who absent themselves from the Abbey...we have paid well to place Winifrith there. The Abbess is known for holding on to her novititates.....Winifrith is still far from her vows, although it is our wish that she should return."

Mistress Keylewey sounded peturbed by this turn of events, although resigned to Winifrith's truculence. She was a sensible woman who understood that the best course of action would be to return Winifrith to the Abbey and try again, but it was sad that the money clearly meant more to the Abbey than the well being of its young girls. It seemed to follow the same path of greed as the Abbey in Sherborne.

"There is just one part of her story which I would like to hear," Sir Tobias told her.

Winifrith was quite willing to retell her story. She and her companion, Imogen, had simply walked out of the Abbey with a group of pilgrims. They were still in their plain novitiate robes and once outside, they separated from the pilgrims and with no essence of hurry, took the road leading through Enmore Green and so out onto the track which led eventually to Sherborne where Winfrith lived. Imogen lived in the little hamlet of Motcombe and was about to part from Winfrith when three masked men confronted them.

At this point in the telling, Sarah Keylewey snorted her disbelief, and Winfrith's eyes filled with tears.

"My lady mother, this is true," she exclaimed. Sir Tobias held up his hand to still the anger bubbling in Sarah's eyes.

"This may well be true," he told her. "Continue, Winfrith." The girl looked at him gratefully.

"The masks were horrible. They had red eyes, snarling lips and horns. The people were on foot and seemed to come from the direction of the forest....I ran...I tripped over and fell. I could see they had grabbed Imogen and I rolled into the ditch. When I looked again, they had gone, but I could still hear them. Imogen was screaming and screaming...I can still hear her in my head...I took off my habit and hid it in the ditch. It was wet through...I was lucky then... a party of travellers came along and I climbed into their cart.... they came all the way to Sherborne, and they didn't ask me anything. I just sat very still and hopped down when they came into town."

"How can this be true?" Sarah Keylewey said, indignant that Sir Tobias was giving credence to her daughter's story.

"Because," said Sir Tobias heavily, "a young girl's mutilated body was found on the edge of the deer pale in Motcombe. She had cropped hair, similar to your daughter ...cropped to discourage vanity and to allow the close fitting coif to be more comfortable. Now I understand where she came from and why the bailiff did not recognize her. I must return to Shaftesbury."

Shaftesbury.

Sir Tobias and William, together with his scribe, left for Shaftesbury early the next morning. It was hardly light as they rode off, it still being only late February. Sir Tobias hoped that the bailiff had done as he had been asked, and had been able to identify the girl, otherwise he himself would have to seek an audience with Abbess Stourton to break the news.

The men rode in silence, anxious to make good time over the sixteen miles. The track was muddy and slippery in places making progress more cautious than they would have liked and the trees which overhung the route in places were bare and stark, forming angular patterns against a grey sky. They met with few travellers and encountered no signs of wandering returning soldiers. A bleak day altogether, Sir Tobias mused.

He allowed his mind to consider the visit to Poyntington Manor....a possible alliance for Lady Alice....a comfortable home....a widowed knight some twenty years older than Alice, but he appeared kind to his household...Luke? Would he send Luke away? Alice would not like that, but it might be necessary....Were there any other options? At present he did not think so, but he had not spoken with Alice...indeed, had not been definite at Poyntington with his intentions although it must have been obvious what was in his thoughts when he visited. There was of course the difficulty of the manner of Allard's death. That had remained in local circles a vague rumour of internal dispute with his men, never questioned and little discussed, but for a new marriage alliance, might need to be explained in a little more detail.

As they approached Shaftesbury he turned his thought deliberately to his mission here. He hoped the bailiff had some idea of the identity of the girl.

In this he was of course disappointed. He was annoyed to discover that the girl had been coffined and buried with the scantest of ceremonies. To the bailiff's credit, he had the grace to look dismayed on hearing what Sir Tobias had to say, and together they approached the Abbey to seek an audience with Abbess Stourton.

The gate to the Abbey was close to the death house where they had initially taken the girl's body, very close to Trinity church. There was a bustle within this gate; the outer area of the abbey held the stables, delivery bays, armoury, for the Abbess was required to send armed men to the king if so required, and ale house and granaries.

Lay folk were about their daily business, all relating to the smooth workings of the inner sanctum of this great nunnery. In this outer area, Sir Tobias discovered, was also the dwelling place of the novitiates and their mistress. He wondered whether he should pause and speak with her, but decided the Abbess should know first the fate of one of her young charges.

As they progressed through the working area into the Abbey itself, guided now by a gatekeeper nun, the pace changed. It became more gracious, a serene gliding peace seemed to permeate...nuns seen through chiselled doorways or arched lintels...such a contrast to the inner halls of this Abbey which thronged with pilgrims, some of whom carried offerings to the shrine. There was chatter here, kept hushed by two nuns whose task it was to organize the line of penitents and pilgrims, all anxious to pay homage and pray by the sacred bones of Edward, King and Martyr.

Certainly the holy relics made much silver for the Abbey for there was evidence of wealth untold in this place. Sir Tobias had not been into the Abbey before, it being a place for women, yet even here men had precedence. There were chantry chapels, each with a priest assigned to pray for the soul of those who had paid for the privilege....and the nuns had father confessors....and only priests could administer the blessed sacrament.

Sister Aurelia kept her pace steady but allowed no pause for staring at the glorious lines of the columns and soaring arched roof space or for wondering about the murmur of prayer which emanated from within. Nor did she attempt any conversation with her visitors. They passed through a cloister leading off the principal part of the Abbey, high altar glimpsed through the rood screen with a crucified Christ and the pyx above lit..... stairs from this passage led upwards to the dortoirs...

night stairs, Sir Tobias supposed, for the nuns to use when they came down to sing their offices during the night watches. Finally they entered the domain of Abbess Stourton. Although simply arranged, every thing about it spoke of the finest quality. It was warm and well lit by an arched window looking out over the valley below and was slightly apart from the main buildings. The walls were adorned with brightly coloured murals....the women at the tomb, the anointing of Christ's feet by Mary, and above the desk hung a jewelled crucifix, the tortured Christ in his final agony.

Abbess Stourton rose as they entered, elegant eyebrows raised in enquiry. Her habit was of the finest wool, perfectly draped around a tall statuesque figure. Long fingered hands were still, resting on the desk in front of her, and the grey eyes which studied her guests showed no trace of alarm. Her oval face framed by her coif and wimple allowed the bones of her cheeks to be well defined. Sir Tobias thought her a handsome woman, despite a certain narrow line of the lips. Sister Aurelia waited with folded hands for her dismissal, head meekly bowed.

"Ask Father Benedict to enter, please Sister," Abbess Margaret directed. To Sir Tobias she said, "You would not expect me to receive two gentlemen without my confessor?"

Sir Tobias and the bailiff waited patiently for the arrival of Father Benedict, who appeared to be an elderly priest with a face which conveyed his suspicion of the two visitors as he settled down demurely on a stool in the corner of the room and folded his hands as if in constant prayer.

"Please be seated, gentlemen. What may I help you with?"

A slightly distant opening, Sir Tobias felt, but he drew breath and studied the Abbess carefully as he began the telling.

"I believe you have two missing novices?" Cool grey eyes looked back at him enquiringly. Sir Tobias continued.

"One of them is the daughter of William Keylewey of Sherborne....she arrived home and is unwilling to return. Her story is of masked men appearing to her, and to her companion...." Abbess Stourton stopped him with a wave of her graceful fingers.

"Always wild tales to excuse inadvisable outings. I would wish her to return."

"Lady Abbess, I believe her companion to be the girl found by the forester, hideously murdered near the old king's hunting lodge....near the hamlet they call Motcombe."

There was a shocked silence in the peaceful room while this strong willed woman struggled to control her emotions in the presence of two men with whom she was not familiar. Father Benedict moved towards her but she crossed herself and held up her hand to stop him.

"God be merciful to her.... I must see her body."

"This bailiff has had her buried, Abbess Margaret."

"We must seek exhumation and give her the proper rites of burial. Why did you do so? What gave you that right?"

The bailiff stammered his abject apologies, refusing to meet her angry eyes.

Sir Tobias told her the story Winifrith had recounted, adding the forester's discovery and the subsequent journey they had made. He did not spare the bailiff either, making it clear that the hasty burial was not what he himself had advised.

It was a chastened bailiff who left the Abbey some time later, aware that an exhumation was to be arranged, and that Abbess Margaret was deeply unhappy with himself and the Shaftesbury coroner. Sir Tobias rejoined William and his scribe and they sought an ale house to refresh the inner spirit and record the conversation with the Abbess.

"If we find the sister and her husband slaughtered thus," William mused. "It is a random selection by men who are crazed. There is an element of devil worship here."

"They may have said or done something to incite the first killing, but it seems as if the young girls were in the wrong place at the wrong time. I intend to keep a watching brief on the case as far as I am able to assist Master Jacobson in his search for his sister and her husband, but at the moment that is as far as I can go."

"Shall we travel down to the forest to seek further sightings of Master Jacobson's sister and her husband while we are here?" William suggested.

So they retraced their journey and came once more to the place where the girl's body had been found. There were still traces of the fire, the ground was scuffed and beyond lay the more thickly forested area.

"I should have realised at once that the girl belonged to the Abbey," the Coroner mused. "Her shorn head should have told me…the coif and cap of their calling is more easily worn with short hair. I did not consider it."

The men hobbled their horses and moved further into the forest on foot. They progressed carefully, seeking a pathway through thick undergrowth, stepping over tangled tendrils from roots, kicking through dead leaves and encountering sucking, marshy ground. At one point they came upon a place where it appeared as if a deliberate pathway had been forged, narrow, but accessible, leading deeper into the silent woods. Here were tall oak trees, devoid now of leaves, but underpinned with thicker ivy, hawthorn, viciously spiked blackthorn and tall bracken, brown and brittle now before the Spring came. The woods held a damp, rotting scent.. ..earthy and slightly unpleasant. Sir Tobias paused, glanced about him to attempt to fix some landmarks before pressing on down the barely discernable pathway they had found. Small marshy streams trickled through the vegetation at intervals, making the ground a sucking uneven surface. The silence surrounding them was deep and slightly sinister. William and the scribe followed, pushing through the network of fern. The vegetation hid the daylight and caused uneasy shadows to fall around them. They pressed on, eager to discover some sign, any sign, of human passage through here.

Although they found none, it was obvious that a way had been forged here so despite the cold they continued to follow this narrow cleft, hoping for success. Eventually, just as Sir Tobias had decided they should retrace their steps before they lost the daylight, they came into a small glade, silent and forbidding. In the middle of this was slight evidence of a fire...a small pile of splintered ash, kicked earth, nothing to speak of...it looked as if someone, either human or animal, had disturbed what was left of the evidence. But a fire... here....in this most deserted part of the forest? It seemed too deep into the forest to be the work of deserting soldiers, struggling home after the unsuccessful wars in France which England was now losing heavily, making way for dissatisfaction and despair. There was nothing else left there....William dug with the tip of his sword but it yielded nothing. Yet it certainly did seem as though a fire had been lit here.

"This could be nothing but soldiers, tinkers, travellers.....but it is odd to have lit a fire so far into this part of the forest."

Regretfully the men decided they must turn back, but it was definitely a place which Ezekiel Jacobson should search for further investigation, although earlier in the day than this, - light was beginning to fade now.

Resolving to call on him without delay as soon as they reached home, Sir Tobias called a halt to their investigation, and they returned to their mounts.

As they retreated, Brother John breathed out with relief. He had been in the hide as they arrived, and his frail heart jumped in fear as he wondered what new atrocities he might have to witness. His hands shook, his heart pounded...he remembered how he had left his patient unguarded although still unconscious...he must not do that again....he just wanted to discover whether any bird song had returned to the place. It had not, and he was about to leave when he had heard the party approaching. He froze as effectively as he was wont to do when observing the wild creatures and his hide had been so expertly constructed that the men had not noticed it in the fading daylight.

He took careful note of the men. He did not dare reveal himself for fear that they were the culprits. He watched the older man.....a face wearied by what? By debauchery and devil worship or by the trials of a life surely spent soldiering, by his stance. He could not risk it...the other two....one definitely war like....he held a sword with which he poked the few dusty ashes. The third man had a satchel round his person....maybe a servant? Brother John held his breath until the noise of their leaving receded into the distance. The woman still lived, but he was not confident enough to leave her yet to summon help. He must protect her from a repeat attack. He would have to stay hidden.

Sherborne

Matthias listened carefully to the account of Sir Tobias. In his experience, limited though it was, devil worship was frightening, evil and often accentuated by hallucinatory herbs, which caused the participants to lose all reason. If it was genuine without the aid of substances, it was deeply unpleasant and involved human and animal sacrifice. The men and women who indulged in such practices could be anyone, hiding their passion for ritual and blood letting behind ordinary outward appearances. He was amazed that such evil could flourish in a town such as Shaftesbury with its Abbey influence so strongly felt all around.

"Flourish is too strong a word, Matthias," Sir Tobias admonished. "It may be confined to just one or two people, but it should be flushed out....and I am not the person to do this. Shaftesbury has its own affairs to look to....I rely on the Abbess and her faith."

Never the less, Matthias agreed to accompany Ezekiel back to the forest to continue the search.....

Winifrith was not at all minded to return to Shaftesbury. The pattern of the great nunnery did not suit her at all, and now she was home, she was resisting return. Pretty things attracted her; young men were drawn to her and she to them and she was dismayed when her father told her he had made arrangements for her to return to Shaftesbury chaperoned by Masters Jacobson and Barton, who were travelling to the area the next day.

William Keylewey felt very fortunate in this. He had met Sir Tobias in Sherborne to thank him for his donation and for his help in taking the news of Winifrith's return to Shaftesbury Abbey. He mentioned his need to return Winifrith to Shaftesbury, and Sir Tobias, on learning that Winifrith was an able rider suggested that she should ride with Matthias and Ezekiel who were travelling there the next day. They would deliver her right to the mistress of novitiates.

Alice and Martin yet again were drawn in to the schoolroom, and Matthias was thankful for the Coroner's forethought in passing on education to his daughter...he was impressed at the cool, competent way she now took his place in the schoolroom.

Alice was surprised to find herself less than impressed when she met Winifrith, mounted prettily on her palfrey and already sizing Matthias up with coquettish glances. William Keylewey delivered her to Barton Holding himself, and intended returning to Sherborne to ready himself for a journey to London with Richard Rochell to attempt to finalize the almshouse licence. He was relieved that Winifrith would be safely back at the Abbey.

Winifrith made sure that she kept close to Matthias during the journey; the track to Shaftesbury was an easy one to ride, and was tolerably wide in places. They paused at an ale house in Henstridge for Winifrith to take her ease in the appropriate place; Ezekiel and Matthias meanwhile relieved themselves at the back of the ale house and on remounting, Winifrith made great play of needing Matthias to help her mount, squeezing his gloved hand with more pressure than he liked.

"Do you wish me to ride further away, Matthias?" Ezekiel asked, roguishly.

"Certainly not...indeed, it seems I may need protection!"

Ezekiel laughed quietly to himself. It was obvious to him that the Keyleweys had a real problem here. He would be glad when they had delivered their charge.

Matthias found himself battered with the girlish prattle of Winifrith. She appeared to feel she had made some impression on Matthias and her shallow chatter washed over him as they rode together, Ezekiel close behind. Matthias found he did not have to answer her, - the words simply rode on and on in a never ending trail.

If the words seemed never ending, so too did the journey. Conversation with Ezekiel was impossible, and silent thought just as impossible. Matthias found himself longing for the straightforward common sense of Alice as a travelling companion.

William Keylewey had told the men to deliver Winifrith to the mistress of novices, inside the gate by Trinity church. They were tired and saddlesore when they arrived, and Winifrith grew silent as they rode through the gate. She slipped down from her mount and stood passively as the mistress of novices came out to meet her.

Matthias took the reins of her horse and looped them through the bridle of his own horse. Master Keylewey had instructed Matthias to ask the master of horse to stable the palfrey until he returned from London, and a groom came shortly and led the beast away. Likewise, the stern faced mistress of novices led Winifrith in, but not before she had embarrassed Matthias by gazing at him and kissing her fingers in his direction. Matthias blushed and dropped his gaze to avoid returning the gesture in any way.

"We could seek rest here for the night," suggested Ezekiel, but Matthias was anxious to leave Winifrith as far behind as possible, so they left and sought beds in one of the many inns abounding in Shaftesbury.

"The girl seems a little simple," Ezekiel ventured, tentatively.

"She certainly does not seem to have her sights set on a holy life style," Matthias agreed, wryly.

Before leaving the town the next morning, Matthias took the opportunity to look around. There was no sign of the bailiff and he did not feel like seeking him out. He found Shaftesbury a pleasing place, although the main market place appeared to be on a steep hill leading down to a lower settlement of houses. There were stocks in the middle of this, unoccupied at present, and the sturdy reinforced battlement wall of the nunnery formed one side of it. On the opposite side were some rather grand houses, glassed windows advertising the wealth of the owners. The great Abbey dominated the town, pushing the commerce towards the Eastern end. There seemed to be a surplus of churches and several market areas although the main one, on what was known as Gold Hill, leading down to the settlement apparently known as St. James, was certainly the busiest. There was a pleasant buzz of humanity here, colourful and vibrant. He guessed the Abbey to be very wealthy, owning much of the town and surrounding pasture land and affording employment to many.

Where he and Ezekiel were bound, however, was not Abbey property, but mostly owned by the King. They collected their horses and set off in the direction of the collection of houses surrounding King John's hunting Lodge, the growing settlement named Motcombe. Passing the small Chapel of Ease with its preachers cross nearby, Matthias paused to wonder whether this was where Martin had grown up. Martin had not told them a name of the village, but he had said it was near Shaftesbury.

Shortly after passing the Chapel of Ease, they branched off onto a narrow footpath, just wide enough to take their horses which would lead them into the forest area.

The meadow leading through the deer pale was criss-crossed by several little streams, and their horses were soon splashed with mud. When the thicker part of the forest began, the two men dismounted, hobbled their mounts and proceeded on foot.

It became more and more dense as they fought their way through untended forest. They lost most of the daylight; there were some animal tracks and occasional trills of birdsong, but it was wet underfoot and unpleasantly so in places. Water dripped off overhanging branches, still bare of leaves for it had rained recently, and here no sun penetrated to dry the vegetation.

They came unexpectedly across a clearing with a broken down chapel to one side. Tired after their untimely scramble through the undergrowth, they sat with their backs to the wall, examining their scratched hands and taking stock of their surroundings.

Out of the forest it did not seem cold, and Matthias closed his eyes, trying to recall their way back through this neglected forest. He guessed they had found a different way through than Sir Tobias had described because they had not passed lakes or ponds, but this was no bad thing he thought, - it meant they were leaving no part of the forest unsearched. He dozed briefly and became aware of someone humming. He looked at the barber-surgeon. Ezekiel met Matthias' eyes, and noiselessly they stood up.

Matthias felt for his dagger, tucked into his belt, and Ezekiel unsheathed his sword.

Cautiously they moved towards the corner of the wall against which they had been resting. Ezekiel slid his hand along the corner and discovered a broken down entrance on the near side. It had a sharp, jagged step where the stones had been broken and they had to take care as they felt their way into this semi ruined place. They must have been heard, for the humming stopped.

Mathias indicated with his hand for Ezekiel to stay out of sight to provide back up if needed...he had no idea whether this was some sort of hide-out for what had been described as devil worshipping. It might be just the place for a coven to make their own.

Grasping his dagger now ready to attack, he stepped further into the ruins and found himself in a semi covered area which led into a small room with the roof still mainly complete. He could see a figure in the room dressed in a friar's robe, roped and knotted at the waist, with hood thrown back. His shoulders were bent with age and his very bearing told of exhaustion. The figure was utterly still, shielding something on the floor.

"Do not come nearer," a thin voice, shaky and weak.

"I have a knife," Matthias replied, steadily. "I shall use it if you attempt to attack me."

"What do you want? Have you come for the woman?" The friar turned to face him, and in the dim light Matthias could see the frailty and fear in his tired eyes.

"What have you done?" Matthias asked him, afraid that this seemingly frail old man was mad and would suddenly produce a killing knife from within his robes.

"I have done nothing but try to save this woman…" began the friar. Ezekiel was through the door with a bound, grasping the frail brother with a grip of iron. His reserve broke; words tumbled from him.

"Where is she?" he rasped. "Tell me what you have done." He shook the old man as if he had been a rat, and the friar slipped out of his grasp onto the floor, revealing the woman lying on the bed behind him.

Ezekiel gasped and threw himself on his knees by the bed, tears flowing down his cheeks unchecked.

"Jenna….Jenna…." He tried to lift her in his arms and then became aware of the heavy bandaging, bruises and lack of responses.

Matthias raised the friar uncertainly in his own arms and looked around for somewhere to rest him. He had fallen into a faint; his eyes were closed and his heart beat was fast. Beads of sweat stood out on his grey face.

"Ezekiel, help me," he said, frightened that the old man would die.

"I cannot," Ezekiel sobbed, "I must tend to my sister."

Matthias didn't realise he had the strength of will to break through Master Jacobson's grief, but his voice grated sternly over the sobs.

"Ezekiel, she is tended and unconscious. You must help me. This brother may not be the perpetrator; he may have saved her life. You have to help me."

Ezekiel recognized the authority in Matthias' tone, lowered his sister back onto her pillow and turned shamefacedly to Matthias, his common sense revived.

"I'm sorry. Of course."

Ezekiel moved his sister gently over, allowing just enough room for Matthias to lower the elderly friar down beside Jenna. He wiped his eyes on his sleeve.

The two men looked down at the two beneath them – Jenna heavily bandaged and still unconscious, and the friar grey of face and limp, although his eyelids were now fluttering weakly. Ezekiel looked round for water of some kind.... ale...wine...anything which might revive him. Tears of relief and shock were still on his face; his hands shook as he found a small pitcher containing water. He wet a cloth from his own bag and wiped the brother's face, helping Matthias to support him until he revived sufficiently to sit unaided.

"This is my beloved sister," Ezekiel murmured, stroking Jenna's bruised face. "I feared I would never see her again. How did she come to be here?"

Brother John uttered a shuddering breath of relief as he realised these were not the men he feared. He tried to stand but found his legs still too weak.

"Rest easy," Matthias advised him. "We can wait for your story. We have been searching for Jenna and Isaac for days."

"Who has tended her?" Ezekiel wanted to know.

Brother John explained tremulously how he had found her and brought her here afraid that the men would return; how he had packed and dressed her wounds finding no signs of awareness in her. She was breathing; there had been no visible movement from her. He had cleaned her when she had need of it and watched over her for signs of life. He had tried to sing quietly to her but nothing penetrated this dense unconsciousness. He had left her once or twice to return to the place in the forest where he had found her, hiding once when three men he did not know came seeking the clearing. Matthias guessed that the men of whom he spoke were Sir Tobias' party.

He said as much to the Brother.

"I did not know whether they were friends or not. I did not dare risk finding out.

I could not leave her long enough to seek help," Brother John explained, a little colour returning to his cheeks. "It will take me several hours of walking to reach the Abbey or Gillingham, to the bailiff there. I was afraid for her safety in case the devils returned."

"The devils?" Ezekiel echoed.

"I have not told you the whole truth of the matter; we started but half way through."

Matthias squatted down on the floor by the paliasse, and Ezekiel knelt by Jenna, clasping one of her cold hands in his, stroking it carefully as he listened in horror as Brother John explained.

"I have built myself a hide from which to observe the forest birds and animals. It is my habit to paint them...I love to recreate them with my inks and paints. It is my solace in my final years." Ezekiel tried to be patient as he listened to Brother John's lengthy narrative. He needed the details pertaining to Jenna and Isaac; equally, Brother John needed to tell his story to help erase some of the details in his mind. He continued, giving full description of the sudden arrival of the masked, naked men, crazed with hysteria, dragging the body of a man behind them, dancing feverishly in their excitement, burning clothing and shrieking undecipherable words all the while, then crashing out of the forest as suddenly as they had arrived, careless of their naked state and apparently forgetting that they had a second victim with which to deal. Brother John had found her in the undergrowth bleeding heavily, badly torn and bruised, still partly clothed. His efforts to move her had opened more wounds, but he had been afraid of the men returning. He had a little wine in his meagre store, so he had used this to cleanse her savage wounds before tearing strips of cloth to bind them. He had made up his own mattress for her, sleeping himself on the ground beside her, and piling whatever he had in the way of coverings onto her. She had been with him for nearly ten days, he calculated.

"My brother in law has died, but my sister still lives…if we can revive her."

"When I was in Italy at the monastery," Matthias volunteered, " a man was brought in one day suffering wounds and bruising such as this. He lay unconscious for nearly two weeks, but when he began to rouse he could not remember who he was or what had happened. The monks cared for him tenderly and eventually he made a partial recovery. I pray this will happen to Jenna."

"It is possible," Ezekiel agreed, still on his knees cradling his sister.

"I have doctoring skills," he told the Brother. "I can tend my sister here in this place until she is well enough to be carried to a safer place, if you will allow me to stay."

Brother John bowed his head.

"We do not know your name," Matthias said, suddenly aware of the strange circumstances in which they found themselves.

"I am called Brother John. I am living out my days here in prayer. My spiritual home is the friary in

Ilchester. My life's work is done. I need peace and contemplation in my last days."

Something about the way in which Brother John said this caused Ezekiel to study the physique of the friar. He guessed the brother knew his days were numbered from some infirmity which he was at pains to hide and hoped he might be able to bring some relief to him as well as to his sister.

Ezekiel was adamant that he would remain here with his sister until she was well enough to be moved; Matthias agreed to seek out an apothecary in Shaftesbury and return with whatever he could. However, when Matthias mentioned that he would also visit the bailiff to report this finding, Brother John became very agitated.

"I have protected this lady and sheltered her. I do not know who these men were, but they came from the direction of Shaftesbury....and you tell me there has been another such death.....I do not wish to bring the devil worshippers right to my door if they should hear of my wherabouts. We must remain hidden."

Matthias and Ezekiel could understand the logic of this, but were cautious in their promises to Brother John.....someone should know of this.

Someone else indeed did know of it. From their hiding place on the edge of the village, two men waited for the third to join them. They caressed their hideous masks as they waited, excited by the knowledge that soon they would have access once again to the delicious fragrance which transported them beyond the realms of poverty and gave them the exhilarating power to do whatever they liked to whom ever they wished. Power gave them energy and energy gave them strength. The ultimate end to their orgy was always oblivion. The excitement this provided was reward enough, but they must take extra care....the Coroner from Sherborne was a danger. They must make no mistake....but the power was addictive and they were unable to stop.

Sherborne

Dame Margaret was pleased with her collection for the almshouse. She had visited many homes in Abbots Fee tithing and provided Richard Rochell with the accounting from her visits. She was surprised how much work was involved in gaining the licence. They had not even considered the actual building of the place yet, nor chosen an architect. First they needed to be sure they could finance it.

She glanced across the Abbey Green towards the Abbey church, scarred at present by evidence of the fire. All Hallows stood behind it, joined on, the offending narrowed entrance still narrowed. It had caused such ill feeling in the town and was now a constant reminder of the quarrel between the Abbot and the townsfolk. It hadn't made Abbot Bradford any the less haughty towards them. She saw him approaching from the direction of the Shambles and deliberately turned into Lodbourne to avoid any confrontation. When meeting him, he never failed to remind her of the debt the town must pay to repair the fire damage.

Before returning to her home at the top of Cheap Street she called in to see Mistress Sarah Keylewey. She was relieved to find that Winifrith had been returned to the Abbey in Shaftesbury, thus freeing William Keylewey to travel to Salisbury, and thence on to London on almshouse business.

"Sir Tobias very kindly arranged for her to be chaperoned by his young friend Matthias Barton and the barber surgeon from Oborne," Sarah told her.

"Winifrith seemed nervous about her return....she did finally seem to appreciate what a narrow escape she had. I wonder sometimes why she is so slow to understand things. Her head is filled with nonsense."

"What does Master Barton do?" Dame Margaret asked.

"He seems to have a small school in Milborne Port.....he was schooled by our own Thomas Copeland who still advises him. I understand he has made quite a small success of the idea. It is good to see younger people assume responsibility."

"I think he is the same young man who attempted to bring Father Samuel's killer to justice," Dame Margaret recalled.

"That was a sad affair," Sarah Keylewey said. "Something to do with the Abbey, I think. It was never really explained fully. Father Abbot chooses not to explain such things."

"He is only interested in explaining how much the town owes him for the fire," Dame Margaret remarked acidly as they parted.

Matthias arrived at Martha Jacobson's home the next day. He was exhausted, having obtained the supplies and herbs needed by Ezekiel. He then had to make a second and a third journey with cloth suitable for bedding which he had been able to take from Jenna's house. To do this he had to call on the neighbour to help him, as Ezekiel had locked the house. This meant of course telling the neighbour part of the story and imploring him to say as little as possible until they were able to move Jenna.

He felt they needed more assistance than Ezekiel realised; he was so shocked at the livid purple bruising round her eyes, the shoulder wound which was deeply slashed and the frail appearance of Brother John, but for the moment, he was resolved to agree not to alert the local bailiff to their presence. Brother John's fear of being sought out if the perpetrators learned that one woman had lived to tell the tale was very real. Matthias also remembered that Sir Tobias had not fully trusted the bailiff.

He had not been to his own home yet, feeling that his first call should be on Martha Jacobson.

She answered the door herself, her face distraught as she realised that Ezekiel was not with him.

"Is my husband taken again?" she cried. Matthias sought to allay her fears immediately.

"No, no...we have found Jenna alive...alive but badly wounded.." Matthias helped her to a chair, where she sat upright, grasping the arms of the chair in agitation.

"Tell me now...quickly before the children come back. They are out walking with my maidservant."

Matthias described the events of the previous day as they had unfolded. Mistress Jacobson listened, becoming calmer as Matthias progressed to the taking of the bedding back to Brother John's cell.

"Your husband will stay with Jenna until he feels she can be moved. I think he will want to bring her here, but the journey will be too long for her. We will need to consider that carefully."

"How can I best help?" Martha Jacobson asked him.

"Give me a change of clothes for your husband,....
I will return tomorrow and deliver them."

"Your school room will suffer your absence,"
Martha said, quietly.

"No," Matthias assured her, "Martin and Lady Alice
will manage. I must see Sir Tobias before I return home.
I will call tomorrow early for the package."

As he rode away from Oborne, Matthias realised
how tired he was, and how weary even his horse had
become. He looked longingly towards his own home as
he ignored the road to Milborne Port and continued to
Purse Caundle.

Sir Tobias heard the story in silence. He took in the
utter weariness of Matthias and called for William.

"It is folly for you to ride over there again tomorrow,
Matthias. You need to have a day without having to
mount, ride and scramble through forest. I know- we
did that journey, or one very like it. We must have been
very near the ruined place. Fetch the package from
Mistress Jacobson as arranged, and then let William go.
He will be able to find the place and he will be fresh – he
can find extra supplies in Shaftesbury if necessary and
take them back to Ezekiel. Meanwhile, I myself will go
and visit Abbess Stourton. I understand the reluctance
to involve the bailiff, but someone should know of this.
William and I will ride most of the way together."

He was glad to have been relieved of the need to ride
again tomorrow and William offered to collect the package
from Mistress Jacobson so they could move off early.

Matthias had never been so pleased to see his own
home as he was on this day. He ached in every bone.
The bedding had been particularly heavy and awkward
to carry, especially as he had needed to leave his horse

before taking to the narrow forest paths. His arms felt weighted down, his thighs were sore from so much riding in the cold and damp and his eyes felt gritty with tiredness.

He slipped from the saddle, afraid his legs would give way. His balance was disturbed and he staggered a little as he looped the reins over the fencepost.

School was over for the day and Alice was waiting for Davy to return from the village to escort her home, together with Luke.

"Thank you, Lady Alice. I shall be in school myself tomorrow."

Alice's face fell a little, disappointed at not being needed in school.

"I am too tired to tell you all we have found...apart from the fact that we have found Jenna alive but badly injured....your father will tell you."

"You are weary and sore, Matthias. Let me fetch some wine to revive you...come through to your own room."

Matthias allowed himself to be led into his comfortable study, where Alice drew out a chair for him and knelt to remove his boots. In a daze, Matthias allowed her to do so, closing his eyes to hide his sudden tears of weariness and relief. Breathing deeply he fought to control the urge to stroke Alice's hair as she knelt in front of him. What a blessing it would be to have such a woman as his wife, someone who would understand his work, share his pleasures and comment on their daily life. He recalled such moments in his parents' lives.... companionable times shared sometimes with himself and his two sisters. His exhaustion made him tearful; unable to speak for fear of appearing weak, he said nothing, folded his hands carefully together and accepted the wine Alice poured for him without a word. She set it on the table beside him and waited for him to recover sufficiently to speak.

"Jenna lives." Matthias made the statement quietly... so quietly that it was difficult to hear him. "Isaac has been murdered. Jenna is unconscious."

"Master Jacobson has stayed with his sister?"

"Yes, William will go tomorrow to take things he needs."

"What else can I do for you, Matthias?"

He opened his eyes at the same moment that the sun shone behind Alice, touching her face with light, showing him a gentle, calm profile, intelligence in her eyes watching him carefully. Her hair, framed by a simple veil, had fallen half loose and trailed over one shoulder. Her lips were parted, generous lips which were beginning to smile again after her trials of last year although at this moment stilled in grief for Ezekiel's news. Her dark blue eyes were wide with concern for his state...he had ridden and walked so far today, backwards and forwards to the chapel where Jenna lay, so that his thighs ached making everything uncomfortable however he sat. He moved restlessly to try and ease the pain, enjoying looking at her with that old feeling of guilt. Alice smiled slightly.

"I think I should leave you, Matthias. You need to rest, sleep and then eat something. Elizabeth will cook for you when you have slept a little."

He so wanted to cry "Don't leave me, Alice" but the words would not form in his throat. It would be so terrible if she was simply being kind. No, he would not be so stupid as to think she would want to stay. Loneliness was his to bear.

Abbot Bradford and his prior were poring over their account books. The repairs to the burned Abbey were eating at Abbot Bradford's soul. He could not rest; he thought about the ruins every day and tried hard to diminish the hot anger within him. As a man of God he knew he should forgive, but he found it very hard to do so. Bishop Neville had been of little help this time, - he was preparing to leave Salisbury and travel to Durham so Abbot Bradford would have to explain the whole sordid story to a new bishop. He prayed daily that the new bishop would be supportive.

"I will commission a stone mason to examine the fallen stones and sort them. Some must surely be usable. The hundred court will demand a work force from the townspeople to assist in the compensation. I have issued a summons against them for wilful damage."

Prior William sighed heavily. His Abbot was a trial to him. It was certainly a fact that the attitude of the Abbot towards the townspeople had done much to exacerbate this whole incident – and Prior William was not convinced that the matter was entirely over.

"You have raised certain taxes, my lord Abbot. Let us examine the accounts closely.

We need to be able to pay the stone mason...even if the townspeople are required to offer us certain hours without payment."

"And they will do so," declared the Abbot, hotly. He broke off, aware that his anger was showing.

Prior William bent over the account books. He calculated the extra taxes imposed on

the market, the mills and the tenements owned by the Abbey.

"Some of these rents can be increased, my lord," he murmured. "We should take care which ones to increase. It is not in our interest to impose more poverty on those who are already struggling to pay."

The Abbot turned his attention to the accounts to which his prior referred.

"What angers me more, Prior William, is the collections being made for the almshouse. The people are willing to donate to that. They have a debt to pay to me first. How can we agree that the citizens are poor when the collection is going from tithing to tithing? I cannot condone or understand it."

"Have you been approached for a donation, my lord Abbot?"

"They would not dare, under the circumstances."

Dame Margaret had other ideas, but she was wise enough to bide her time.

Shaftesbury.

William approached the ruined chapel carefully. Like the previous parties, he had to leave his horse hobbled before heading on foot into the forest. The path was a little dryer today and the bracken and undergrowth had been brushed aside by Matthias quite roughly so a narrow path was starting to emerge.

He called out softly when he was near enough to prevent startling the party. Ezekiel emerged from the door, looking tired and dishevelled. There were dark rings under his eyes and lines of weariness visible in his face.

"Thank you." He took the package of clothes Martha had sent, and ushered William inside. He noticed Brother John was quietly praying in an inner room where there seemed to be a makeshift altar. The two men conversed in hushed voices allowing Brother John his peace and solitude.

William explained that Martha had sent clean clothes and he himself had brought food and wine, and warned Ezekiel that Sir Tobias was visiting Abbess Stourton to inform her of events, not fully trusting the bailiff.

Ezekiel gave William details of Jenna's injuries. He could see for himself that she was still unconscious although the bruises were beginning to turn from purple to a livid yellow. The shoulder wound was ragged as though she had been dragged along a blade in haste. Ezekiel had opened it and cleansed it of pus and matter and would do so again if he felt it necessary. However she had no fever now so he hoped with time and patience she would rouse.

"I find it amazing," declared William, "that both Martin and Jenna have received deep wounds and yet no infection has set in. On the battlefields so many men succumbed to infection with wounds less deep that Martin's...and Jenna, too."

"In Martin's case, the amputation was cauterised immediately, and when he was slashed so viciously in the barn, we were quick with the wine, the egg white, the mallow. He did have a little fever for a while, after the first stitching, but we beat it.

In Jenna's case I think we have just been lucky. Brother John moved her away from the forest quickly and he has some little knowledge of cleansing....it is cleansing that is so important. Not everyone agrees, but I was taught that very early. I have observed barber surgeons treating patients without washing their hands, with dirty instruments and with over-used and dirty cloths to bind wounds. It just takes a little care to prevent infection."

"We have been fortunate to find you," William told him.

Sir Tobias was seated in the cool hall outside the Abbess' room. Her time was taken at present by another matter, and he was able to look in appreciation at the wall paintings, the floor tiles, the glassed windows of this part of the Abbey.

His guide through the Abbey grounds this time had been a nun of great age and even greater tongue! She had chatted to him freely as they crossed the courtyards and entered the abbey church, passing pilgrims gossiping together as they waited for their turn.

"We are having the blessed bones of Edward, King and Martyr transported to a new crypt," explained the old nun, "the pilgrims are many and often quite excited to be here, so we need to have a proper place for them to go so we can once again enjoy the tranquillity of the Abbey."

Sir Tobias was amused that she should be speaking of tranquillity in such a loud voice, and so vociferously.

"Where will that be?"

"Oh, to the North of the Abbey, to be sure...and down steps, to ensure the pilgrims are directed away from the main part of our Abbey. They are too noisy. The building will begin soon."

She left Sir Tobias waiting in the whitewashed hall, noises of the Abbey muted now.

Two nuns emerged from the room after a while, eyes downcast. Sir Tobias imagined they had been reprimanded. From his impression of Abbess Stourton so far, she would be strict.

He knocked lightly on the door.

"Come!"

He entered. Father Benedict, her confessor was present, as he had been the last time, and she herself looked as if she had not moved from her place....hands steepled together, long graceful fingers, clear grey eyes regarding him steadily from her alabaster face framed by her coif. The words were the same, too.

"How may I help you?"

Sir Tobias began his tale. He expressed his distrust of the bailiff, his own willingness to search for Jenna and Isaac to support Ezekiel Jacobson, the return of Winifrith to Sherborne with her tale of masked men, the discovery of the mutilated body of Imogen and finally the search instigated by Matthias and Ezekiel which resulted in finding Jenna and realising that Isaac was dead. He mentioned the fear of Brother John who was convinced that there was some form of devil worship practiced which might result in his place of retreat being found and desecrated and Jenna being reclaimed. Abbess Stourton listened in silence.

"I cannot keep this from the bailiff. What gives you the feeling of mistrust?"

"A man who arrests a stranger for murder with no evidence of bodies is a strange man to appoint as bailiff. He apparently made his accusations without thought. Then there is the matter of the non appearance of the coroner when called for. When he appeared it was too late, and he was too drunk to attend to the matter. Why did he not obey my instructions regarding the identification of the girl? He wished to sweep the entire matter away."

Abbess Stourton appeared to be thinking, - or maybe praying. She did not answer immediately. Father Benedict sat immobile, his face blank.

"How practical might it be to have the woman carried here to our infirmary?" Sir Tobias thought of the journey through the tangled forest.

"Difficult, but not impossible with care."

"She would be protected here and well tended. Once she is safely here, I will summon the bailiff and lay the bones of the tale bare."

"It will be several days before we can bring her," Sir Tobias explained. "We will need to arrange man power and a sling for the lady....two men will be required to carry the sling until we reach the point where we can use other means of transport."

"So be it. The Abbey will provide man power and a horse with a covered waggon. Organize what you have to do."

She summoned the almoner nun to make arrangements for the admission to the infirmary, and provided written authority for the provision of transport as soon as Sir Tobias had made suitable plans. Standing outside the magnificent Abbey looking out over the early Spring countryside below him, Sir Tobias hoped they would be able to bring Jenna to safety.

Sherborne

Martin Cooper was making good progress with his prosthetic. It was now early March; he knew he must make his own way in life very soon and so was keen to follow all instructions given by Master Jacobson carefully. He was sparing with the salve he had been given and tried his limb daily, learning to balance with greater and greater confidence as the days went by. He still used the crutches when walking out of the house; he had not yet had the confidence to balance and weight bear on the new leg.

He had an idea which he wanted to discuss with Lydia, who had become his friend over the few months he had been in Milborne Port, so he had braved the fresh early March wind to walk to her cottage.

He knew he had some skill with wood and he was beginning to understand his shortcomings regarding employment. Lydia listened as he outlined his plans to her....to begin to offer himself as a small time carpenter ....perhaps starting with a commission for just one person who would then recommend him to another.

"I need a patron, Lydia," he suggested, then felt shy at having said such a thing. How could he, partially sighted, expect a patron to offer him sufficient work that others would notice.

Lydia regarded him silently. He was very different from Ben, her late husband, but he was able to make her laugh and she felt comfortable in his presence. She was under no illusions about his strength....he had tired himself out on the walk here, but he was clearly determined to make some sort of new life for himself. Martin had performed several repairs and improvements to the cottage, made a beautiful cot for Freya and Ennis and Freya enjoyed his carving of toys for them. How could she help?

"I'm sorry Martin, I would miss you if you had to move on...but I am not lettered...I can think of no-one who could help you. Why not speak of this to Master Barton. He has been a good friend to you – and to me."

"But you don't think it a foolish idea?"

"I think the things you have made are perfect. Once somebody has seen your work I am sure you would increase in popularity; it helps that the people round here have become accustomed to seeing you."

He touched her hand hesitantly. "Thank you, Lydia. I need some courage to do this, and your praise gives me confidence."

Later, Lydia remembered with pleasure the touch of Martin's hand. Her life would be poorer if he left....she was easy with him, relied on the little things he noticed that he could do for her and thought how changed he had become since the day when she had moved his broken crutch nearer to him with her foot, pity for a fallen beggar moving her from her own unresolved grief. He had been through much in the past year but she never heard him complain. Yes, she would miss him.

Martin ate with Davy and Elizabeth, Matthias usually eating alone, but this evening, Matthias chose to join them in the kitchen, listening to Martin's ideas for his future.

He was diffident in explanation, unsure of his place in the community. Milborne Port was a good sized village and Martin had no wish to impose himself on the tradesmen already established. There were guilds being formed, industries gathering momentum and families who had been at the forefront of village life for many years. He was familiar to most people now, but still not part of their lives. There was a definite line of succession among the tradespeople, and Martin realised he had no place in that.

So how to proceed?

"Where was your home originally, Martin?"

"A small village near Shaftesbury... Motcombe. It is between Gillingham and Shaftesbury. I lived with my mother, but she left whilst I was in France. The house was in poor repair when I returned...in fact, it was burned one night while I was sheltering there."

He recalled his time there with dread. He had crawled into the dilapidated house, now hardly more than a hovel, and curled up in a corner of the one room, the earthen floor damp and rough. It was dark; he could hear the rain beating on the damaged door and he had huddled further into the corner, the semi healed stump of his leg throbbing as if his whole leg was still there. He had slept fitfully and was woken by voices. He could not see who these intruders were....his blinded eye made vision very difficult....but something in their furtive whispered conversation prevented him from making himself known to them. He lay still in the corner, no more than a bundle of rags. There was an argument going on, he remembered. He heard snatches of words... there appeared to be mention of potions, visions, excitement, power, secrecy. Something changed hands for silver he seemed to think...and then there was talk of fire being the essential element...fire gave power.... fire spoke of strength...fire was a necessary end to the rite...the voices drifted away but Martin soon realised that they had left fire burning behind them as a token of their power... a fire which threatened to reach him in his dark corner unless he moved quickly. He had crawled out of the house and taken shelter under a hedge until morning, which is when he resolved to return to see Sir Tobias.

"You would not consider it worth returning there and taking possession of your mother's deserted house?" Davy suggested.

Martin swallowed hard before giving voice to his memories. He had blocked them from his mind, but as he retold them he wondered whether this might have some bearing on the happenings Matthias had been investigating with Ezekiel Jacobson.

"Did you see the fire when it became light?" Matthias asked him, curious now to find out more.

"Yes...the rain stopped the fire from burning everything...there were still some sticks of furniture in the house and I picked one or two things to bring with me...my few possessions meant I felt I was still a person. The neighbours did not like my mother...she was known as a gossip....she took her chances with a traveller they told me. There seemed nothing for me in that place....no point in being there. It was my lowest point. The men I heard in the night had left nothing but ashes."

"You've come a long way and done much since then, almost a rebirth from those ashes." He tried to remember that the conversation was about Martin's future, but he felt a tingle of excitement concerning the incident recalled. What a chance that they had awakened Martin's memories by just discussing his plans for the future!

"I would like to retell your story to Sir Tobias when he returns; it may give Ezekiel a lead in discovering the fate of his relatives."

"Is there still such a thing as devil worship?" Elizabeth asked, fearfully. It sounded dark and sinister to her, living in relative comfort and security.

"Oh indeed there is," Matthias assured her, "but less than there was years ago. There are still warlocks and witches in some parts of the country with sacrificial rites and followers. The covens are often secret and have their own meetings, sometimes held in deserted houses or churches. There were many villages deserted following the plague…that opens up places where such followings can take place."

His words cast a chill over the room, the flickering candles suddenly casting weird shadows.

"Hold fast to your faith, Elizabeth. We have no such evidence hereabouts. Martin, how would it be if I ask some of the parents of our pupils if any of them might have need of work? They know you, you have assisted in the schoolroom…they may provide just the opening you are waiting for."

Martin was content with the suggestion; Matthias was anxious to talk to Sir Tobias as soon as he was home, and Elizabeth felt somewhat reassured of their safety.

Shaftesbury

Shaftesbury was far from safe, however. The darkness of the night hid the darkness of the soul. They met in secrecy, already excited by the burning of the strange roots they had purchased, inhaling the intoxicating fumes with increasing pleasure. The leader had drunk deeply of the wine infused with forbidden fruits, leading to nightmare imaginings which both terrified and exhilarated him. He passed the cup round to the assembled coven, urging them to drink. As they did so, the hoarsely whispered chant grew stronger and stronger…."In the name of Satan…Lucifer…Lord of all darkness…in the name of Satan…Lucifer, the fallen one…"

They joined hands to strengthen their bond. Hands gripped hands…strength flowed round the circle….the leader broke away groaning with lust. He must find a woman...fast....any woman. As he left he grabbed hold of his mask lying on the ground beside him fitting it clumsily over his head. He was ready for anything now...but first to find a woman.

Annastese left the home of her newest mother, delivered of a baby boy after much travail. She was tired; The darkness did not frighten her; there was a weak moon which helped her negotiate the stony track wending up hill; she was known in this community where she worked as a midwife to many young women so slipping out at night was not foreign to her. She picked up speed as she left the house, anxious to lift her own latch and slide into bed beside her husband. Her own children were sleeping beside their bed, all in the one room.

A sudden movement startled her. A roar of rage, unformed words, something evil flying through the darkness towards her....it all happened so quickly. Strong hands gripped her throat; the screams inside her head were strangled before they could be given voice.... hands fumbled roughly up her skirts...she was pressed to the ground becoming conscious of hideous features...a horned head with strange bulbous eyes looming towards her with hideous intensity. Mercifully she lost all feeling before the cruel desecration of her body began.

Sir Tobias was able to make arrangements with the Abbess for moving Jenna more quickly than he expected, and he was on his way to the ruined cell of Brother John at Cowridge to facilitate the transfer. He rode down the hill into Enmore Green where he encountered a knot of people, encircling some local happening. He became aware of women weeping, of some-one's frantic sobbing, of an aura of shock. He dismounted as he saw the body of a young woman with blood soaked and torn clothes. As he drew closer he recognized the unmistakable signs of rape with the now familiar vicious slashes across her upper body.

"Good people...let me through. I am the Coroner for Dorset...."

The small crowd drew back respectfully apart from the older woman who was cradling the dead body of the woman in her arms, heedless of the blood soaking into her own clothes.

Sir Tobias knelt, gently eased the woman's hands away from the body and beckoned to a villager to take the distraught woman further away.

He pulled the clothes down to hide the nakedness between her thighs, noted slight warmth still in the poor body, closed her eyes and was relieved when the priest came panting up from the bottom of the hill, murmuring the words of absolution and blessing even as he crouched on the ground beside the Coroner.

"Who is she?" Sir Tobias demanded of the priest.

"Sir, she is the local midwife. She is called Annastese. She had been with a birthing all night."

"A birthing?"

The priest spoke thickly, lips too dry with horror to enunciate clearly.

"A good woman, sir, young but skilled. 'Twas her own mother who taught her the skills; 'twas her own mother grieving." The sudden tears on the priest's face told of her place in this little village community.

"Carry her to your chapel," Sir Tobias commanded, quietly. Two young men stepped forward and lifted the body carefully. The grieving mother shrieked and tried to throw herself on the body as they raised her. Sir Tobias caught her in his arms and held her close to allow the girl to be moved. She collapsed into him, sobbing, beating her fists against his chest, choking with her grief.

An older man emerged from the crowd and took her from Sir Tobias, stroking her hair and supporting her as she made to follow the corpse.

"Jared must be told," someone said.

"Who is Jared?"

"The husband of Annastese...working in the quarry...he would have left for work before dawn."

Sir Tobias allowed a neighbour to fetch the husband from his place of work, then proposed an examination of the corpse.

"We have our own coroner here in Shaftesbury," a surly voice in the crowd said. "Let's fetch him. We don't know this man."

Sir Tobias scanned the crowd of villagers, picked out the swarthy young man who had spoken, noted his sullen objection but continued with his decision.

"Fetch your own coroner, to be sure. I will wait here until he arrives."

As Sir Tobias waited, the crowd began to disperse until there were only a few near neighbours remaining. After what seemed an age of waiting, Sir Tobias ordered the body to be carried into the nearby chapel unable to linger any longer for the coroner to appear, first speaking to the small group, mostly shocked women, who were gathered around, wanting some action.

"I have had serious conversation with Abbess Stourton regarding the killings here in the King's forest. This is the third one. I suspect no-one here, but I will need to see that questioning is carried out by the local bailiff and your own coroner, when he arrives. I was on my way to bring another badly wounded victim to safety when I chanced upon your midwife."

Sir Tobias was anxious to reach the Cowridge Cell, but first he made a cursory examination of the corpse, lest the coroner should be in the same condition as he had been before. He learned that Mistress Annastese had left some time in the darkest hours of the night to return to her own home, the birthing satisfactorily completed. She lived only a short distance up the hill, near the springs which provided water for Shaftesbury. The birthing had taken place at the very bottom of the hill so she had not far to go, and she was familiar with the track. He found her upper body injuries very similar to those he had seen on Imogen, and from the description of Matthias, also on Jenna. He was suddenly surprised at the length of time it was taking the coroner to arrive.

"Your Bailiff and coroner...do they have far to travel?" he asked the priest. As he spoke he heard the sound of horses, and within moments the door was pushed open and the coroner was scowling at him.

"You again!"

"I would have some respect, coroner."

"My lord Coroner" this with a cursory nod and a sneer.

"I would ask you to examine very thoroughly. Something quite evil is happening here; we need to bring it from darkness into the light, with God's help."

"No need, Sir Coroner. We have arrested the woman's husband. We work fast in Shaftesbury."

There was a shocked cry from the little crowd of women. The coroner scowled at them.

"Jared is the obvious suspect. We have sent to the quarry to arrest him lest he flee."

"Who brought you the news of this death?"

"News travels fast in Shaftesbury. We are not known for delaying. Our felons do not escape justice. He will hang for this."

"No,coroner. This must have more detailed examination. I ask you to pause and consider, - no, more than that, in the name of the King, I order you to pause and examine this in the light of the other killings. Our King is known for his saintly and pious nature. He would not wish to learn of evil and ungodly happenings which were not being pursued by those in authority."

There was a murmur of assent and approval from the women; the coroner glared at Sir Tobias, hot hate in his eyes.

"I shall be in this area for a day or two, coroner. See to it, please. I also intend to hear from the husband Jared."

Sir Tobias remounted his horse and left, unwilling to impose his authority on this most truculent local coroner.

Master Jacobson was pleased to see Sir Tobias emerge from the forest path. Like the others, he had left his horse half way, finding it easier to make his way through the dense overgrown woodland on foot. The king's foresters and verderers were not so many now, working the forest nearer to the old lodge where assarting had taken place. Oak and ash grew well tended, sometimes pollarded, in the acreage nearer to the growing village. Here, where the land was nearer to the border with Mere the undergrowth was more dense and untended. Good poaching was to be had nearer the better tended areas, so the Cowridge Cell had remained undisturbed, allowing Brother John the solitude he craved.

Jenna had stirred a little, moaning with pain, and Ezekiel was anxious that she should receive some numbing potions as she regained consciousness. The removal to the Abbey in Shaftesbury was not going to be easy, but he could see that it would be far better for her than lying out here in this half ruined place.

Brother John was proving to be an easy host, spending much of his time in prayer, moving around quietly seeking to find simple remedies to ease the superficial discomfort of bruising, sharing his simple meals with Ezekiel and showing him some of his drawings of the forest birds and animals. Ezekiel was pleased to be able to see such things, taking his mind away from the abominations of the forest and concentrating on the beauty and simplicity of the freshness depicted.

Sir Tobias appreciated that their journey to Shaftesbury might well be interrupted rudely, even violently, since it had been impossible to remain entirely confidential. He was mindful of the sullen faced man in the crowd who had objected to his involvement. Was it he who had taken swift word to the coroner and so caused the arrest of Jared? And why would he have done such a thing? Was there protection of a murderer in the crowd at Enmore Green? There could have been a word spoken out of place unwittingly by Jenna's neighbour or even a nun speaking out of turn in the presence of a lay worker with a hand in this spate of devil worship. He was eager to make this difficult journey before any harm befell them.

To achieve this end, they were somehow on the track by dawn the next day, William and Ezekiel carrying

Jenna in the sling between them, and Sir Tobias following. Brother John led the way, knowing the easiest route to follow. He was reluctant to leave his cell for so long but he understood the need for speed, especially as Jenna was slowly beginning to regain consciousness. He grasped his stave firmly as he walked, aware of his encroaching infirmity but determined to show none of it. He was to go with them as far as the wagon which was meeting them at the crossing of Cusborne Lake, close to the area known as Coppleridge. Then he would return to his home and attempt to put this incident behind him.

The thrashing of sticks against undergrowth echoed through the forest. There was nothing secretive about this; the vigorous, angry thrashing continued, beating a wider path than had been there before. They passed through the clearing where the fire had been which had burned Isaac and thrashed through the hide without fully realising what it was, further and further on. Eventually they came to a ruined building, signs of life apparent. Theirs was no silent approach on this day. Their angry voices exclaimed at the sight of habitation. There were boots which kicked, sticks which laid into simple pots and utensils. Finally there was the utter desecration of the altar, holy psalter trampled, torn pages, boot marks on sacred items. Panting with exertion and with eyes wildly flashing, the coven swore on oath that whoever had made his home here would be given the same treatment as others.....but now they must return to their work for fear of being missed. This would have to wait.

His part of the task completed, Brother John returned through the forest to his home.

He noticed with trembling limbs the disturbed bracken beaten and crushed, making the pathways wider and messier but there was no sound to alarm him. Despite this, the devastation of his carefully kept cell came as an unpleasant shock. It stopped his breath as he studied the ruined coverings, made his unsteady heart beat unevenly, drained the blood from his head. He clutched the wall, taking a cautious and unsteady step. When he reached his inner room and understood the extent of the damage, he crouched down, keening softly for the destruction of his very faith in God.

By nightfall the cell was empty, a shell for the wind to blow through, erasing all memories.

Sherborne.

Sir Tobias returned to Sherborne once Jenna was safely delivered to the Abbey infirmary. William and Ezekiel accompanied him. The Abbess had been quite clear concerning the place of men in her Abbey – not negotiable. There were priests as part of the Abbey – there had to be – only priests could celebrate the blessed eucharist and people paid chantry priests to pray for the souls of their relatives. In fact, Ezekiel would arrange a chantry priest in the future to pray for Isaac, although most likely at St. Peter's. Abbess Stourton had been more than content to allow Ezekiel to speak with the infirmarian who would be caring for Jenna with all due care. She was showing slight signs of movement now; Ezekiel had joined the line of pilgrims snaking towards the bones of Edward the martyr and given thanks for his sister, prayed for her recovery and given thanks for the nuns.

Sir Tobias had called on the bailiff to establish that the enquiry into the murder in Enmore Green was progressing and that Jared had been released from arrest. There were children to care for and Jared's grief and shock were testament enough to discredit the belief that he had somehow been involved in the death. The bailiff and coroner were clearly angry at the interference of Sir Tobias, but his seniority and threats to send a messenger to the King were enough to secure Jared's release – at least for now. He intended to return to Shaftesbury after dealing with business in Sherborne. He did not entirely trust that matters in Shaftesbury would be adequately dealt with.

There were several small incidents in the surrounding area of Sherborne needing the Coroner's attention, so he took his scribe with him and went to his usual place in The George Inn to hear details prior to deciding whether these should go on to the hundred court or be dismissed.

The cases were small but seemed numerous; blocking the path with rubbish, arguing with a neighbour to frighten other neighbours within hearing, stealing a cloak from an old woman, fighting outside an ale house, - and then a little more serious – selling underweight bread, short ale measures. These needed more attention from the hundred court.

He was surprised to receive a visit from Abbot Bradford as he was packing up his belongings and preparing to return home. The Abbot was wearing his normal supercilious expression as he seated himself in front of the Coroner, but he tried hard to sound and look less so.

"This conversation must needs be confidential," began Abbot Bradford, suddenly hesitant. Sir Tobias bowed his head in acknowledgment.

"I have a baby to dispose of," announced the Abbot. "It has been delivered to the Abbey by an angry father of a local girl and left with us. We cannot care for the child. The discipline will be dealt with internally but I wish to place the child in a safe home. I admit our rule has become careless and in certain cases morally lax. It is my God given duty to attend to the discipline of monks within my care. I accept that responsibility, but we need help in seeking an immediate refuge for the babe."

For this most haughty of Abbots to admit such a failing was unheard of, and Sir Tobias was taken aback, striving to hide his surprise, and if he was honest, amusement. However, he did not know the community of Sherborne well. He was unwilling to involve his own family who lived outside the town. He thought rapidly.

The only public spirited person he knew was Dame Margaret Gough, and he was but thinly acquainted with her. However, he agreed to speak with her.

"The lady is one who was instrumental in the business of the font?" queried the Abbot. Sir Tobias gave him a dry smile.

"You cannot afford to be selective, my Lord Abbot. I am sure the lady will treat the matter in confidence. She appears to know many people within the town." With that, the Abbot had to be content.

Sir Tobias lost no time in seeking out Dame Margaret. She too seemed faintly amused by the Abbot's problem, but also concerned regarding an innocent babe with no protection.

"There is one family who may be pleased to take such a gift," she told him. "Mistress Amice has lost three babes at birth…too weak to survive. They are not a wealthy couple, but they have sufficient on which to live. The husband is an honest man. He works as a quarryman and Mistress Amice takes in needlework. They have a small house in Hound Street, rented from the Abbey. There might well be negotiations available for rent reductions in return for taking the babe. Let me go and see them now. They have lost hope of producing a healthy child."

Sir Tobias remained at The George, pondering the muddle of events which had overtaken him in the previous weeks and months. He wondered afresh whether he should go and visit the manor at Poyntington once more, with a view to a marriage alliance for Lady Alice. Then the strange events in Shaftesbury, affecting the good barber surgeon Ezekiel Jacobson and the daughter of William Keylewey who had surely escaped a gruesome death at the hands of a coven of devil worshippers. What of the other deaths in Shaftesbury, and the incompetence or laziness of the Shaftesbury bailiff and coroner? It was a miracle that Jenna had survived the attack which had killed her husband, due to the solitary friar Brother John who had carried her to safety. What to do now, he wondered, heavily.

First things first, he decided. Poyntington. Lady Alice's future should be secured.

Dame Margaret returned. She came alone, but the news was encouraging. Mistress Amice would take the child at once, on the understanding that it was a trial period and that Dame Margaret would undertake negotiations with Abbot Bradford if there was any future for the child. This arrangement suited Dame Margaret very well. She had a nice little handle on Abbot Bradford now.

Matthias was relieved to be in his own schoolroom once more, organizing the work, advising the scholars of their errors and celebrating their successes. He looked over work done by Alice, assisted by Martin and felt reassured by what he perceived. He had eight pupils now, one of whom was Luke, Alice's son. Soon he would be old enough to join Thomas Copeland's school in Sherborne. That was what was intended, he knew. He had not yet had opportunity to speak to any of the fathers of his charges to make enquiries on Martin's behalf, but he was looking for the chance to do so. He sensed that Martin was becoming uncomfortable about his continuing use of the barn as his home so he determined to ride out with the boys that afternoon when lessons finished to speak with any who met their sons in person.

Matthias had made arrangements for the younger boys to be accompanied to the guildhall in Milborne Port by his man Davy and met by a member of their own household. Two of them came from outlying villages, and it was not safe or sensible for seven or eight year olds to be unaccompanied. In this changing world, they were not well born enough to be placed in the household of a relative to learn the duties of a page, receive private tuition and eventually take their place in some titled position. They were sons of rising merchants, desirous of education to better their chances in this country which appeared to offer them an opportunity to rise in commerce and to one day equal those who considered themselves their betters.

Matthias was fortunate today. Daniel de Thame was a mercer who had business in Sherborne and had stopped on his way home in Milborne Port to wait for his young son, also called Daniel. Matthias had brief conversation with him concerning his son's progress and then succinctly explained Martin's position. Master de Thame was interested, and at once proposed that Martin should make him a new sign for his shop front. It was a simple task, but it was a start, and after hearing what type of sign Master de Thame wanted, Matthias returned home, pleased with his first commission for Martin.

It was now March, and becoming lighter in the evenings. Matthias was startled to observe Lady Alice's palfrey tethered in the yard. He entered the schoolroom to discover her there, standing uncertainly by the work Luke had done that day. Matthias was suddenly nervous of her close proximity and the absence of her maid. He was reminded too clearly of his shame in Paris and the death of the unnamed prostitute from whom he had extracted the news of Allard's death. What happened next was sudden and unexpected.

She turned to face him, breath coming unevenly, her face flushed. Words tumbled from her with no regard for her position. "My father has arranged to take me to Poyntinton tomorrow with a view to arranging a marriage.....Matthias, ...save me from this hell.... I know of no-one else to turn to...."

Matthias was stunned. He stared stupidly at Alice, shaking now with the enormity of what she was asking. There were no sobs....her eyes were dry.....she was looking to Matthias for her salvation. Matthias felt helpless. He could not speak for fear of his voice breaking with emotion, but he knew he could not do as she was asking.

Alice held out her hands to him in supplication. "Matthias, I cannot bear it....to be pawed by an old man.....to be bedded for a son ......to be parted from Luke who is my reason for living.....Matthias, please...."

Matthias had never heard such intimate words from a woman....had not considered how a woman could feel such revulsion.....in that moment he felt too shamed to respond to her.

"I grew to love Allard.....I would have followed him to France when he first went to battle...but he has killed any feeling in me except for my beautiful little boy. I am nothing but discarded womanhood. Now even my father wants to dispose of me..." her voice rose as she fought for control.

"Alice, I cannot help you to avoid what your father has decided," Matthias began.

Did he really know what she was asking him? Was she asking him to wed her or was she asking him to intercede with her father? He did not have the courage to ask. Alice's self control broke. She flung herself against Matthias, beating her clenched fists against his chest in a sudden torrent of weeping.

"You have no feeling, no imagination, no emotion..." she sobbed. Matthias grasped her wrists and detached himself from her. He held her at arms length from himself but found he had no words for her...his throat constricted with pity and something which he thought he might recognize as love.

It was as if a dam had broken in Alice.

"Men have such an easy life...you can go where you please, do what you want, dally with whomsoever you desire.....whilst I am confined.....confined to begging for help from you, the only man I know...you, who are cold unbending and emotionless...but I beg from you..... standing in front of you, shameless in my need....and you will not help me. Can you not imagine how it will feel to go to the bed of someone who is old, repulsive, dribbling, incontinent, intent only on a brief moment of pleasure? You cannot hope to understand the excitement and pleasure of lying in the arms of someone who makes every part of you tingle with sweet desire..... I have felt it for a short time. It was wonderful while it lasted but when Allard did not look back as he rode off after Luke was born I felt a heavy sadness in me. My happiness transferred to my son...Matthias.. I will lose my son if someone does not help me..." she was becoming more rational as she continued.

Matthias found some voice, took tight control of his own emotions, tried to think sensibly. Alice had expressed her need for help; she had not mentioned love, respect, even fondness. What was it she wanted? What was it he wanted himself? She had called him cold, unbending, emotionless. Was he all those things? He remembered the nights of desparing tears he had shed after his family had been so devastated by sickness, the cold courage he had summoned to leave England behind as a young man... had that been courage or cowardice? He looked at Alice, calmer now. She would have left, but he took her by the sleeve and propelled her to a seat. When she was calm he made a decision, hoping his voice did not shake too much.

"I cannot go against your father's wishes," he repeated, "but I will come home with you now and ask your father to consider allowing you to become a partner in this school." He wondered at himself even as he uttered the words. Where had they come from? He had not considered the proposition at all...it had just burst from his head on the spur of the moment. How would he afford it? Would he be required to offer a salary? Would Sir Tobias even hear what he had to say?

"You are a good teacher, Lady Alice. You have much to offer. I would enjoy working with you. I'm sorry if this sounds cold and unbending – I know no other way to say this. I love my work with the boys and together we can look to increase their learning." Matthias was terribly aware that his words sounded priggish and distant, but he was fighting his inner desire to take Alice in his arms and hold her tightly to reassure her that she was far from being discarded were suddenly very strong. He must not do that. She had not spoken of affection. He felt Sir Tobias would not accept such a union and he must never deceive himself that it could come about. He recalled the first time he had seen Lady Alice – and the feelings it had aroused in him. He set himself to forget that time. She had asked for help...salvation...she had not mentioned love. He would not do so either. Let it be a business arrangement.

Matthias was good as his word. He accompanied a subdued Lady Alice to Purse Caundle and sought a private interview with Sir Tobias. He did not see Lady Alice when he left, - and he was not clear whether his proposition would be acceptable. It was a very unusual suggestion and would allow Lady Alice to remain with Luke and within her own family, doing work she enjoyed.

His heart was sore as he rode home in the gathering dusk; the opportunity had been presented to him but he had not taken that path. He recognized in himself an increasing craving for love, acceptance and deep friendship. He had fallen for Alice from the very first time he saw her but had suppressed his feelings, knowing her to be a married woman. Now she was free he felt burdened by guilt knowing how he had obtained the information about the death of her husband....and remembering how

sudden and urgent had been his physical need....but the
final nail had been supplied by Alice herself; she wanted
salvation, protection and the assurance that she would
still have Luke with her, not love, passion and companionship, That was incompatible to Matthias and not the
right basis for a marriage in his view. It seemed as incompatible as Alice being wedded to an old man for the sake
of security.

He sighed as he reached his home, which felt emptier
to him than it had for some time.

Shaftesbury.

News of Jenna's survival from the murderous attack had
filtered into the town once Abbess Stourton had informed
the bailiff. There was anxiety amongst the townspeople
who knew that a novice had suffered horribly, and that
the midwife from Enmore Green had been killed. There
was support for Jared who had been released, albeit
reluctantly by the bailiff. Neighbours rallied round to
help with the children, to bring dishes of pottage for
supper and to reassure Jared that the killer would surely
be caught. People glanced furtively from one to another,
wondering who amongst them could be indulging in
devil worship. Such a thing had not been known in
Shaftesbury, although the church taught that such a thing
existed and was evil. Mothers kept a close eye on
children, fathers demanded to know where their sons
were and husbands were closely protective of wives. The
sense of evil hung over the town. Jared kept his three
children close by him at all times.

The bailiff slouched in his untidy official domain
adjoining the guildhall, pushing his seal around

aimlessly on what passed as a desk. The shadow of St. Peter's church fell over him as he glared at the tithing men he had summoned.

He was a short, sallow faced man, his eyes set rather closely together. A scar down one side of his neck spoke of experience in battle of some kind. He had an unfortunately large nose, thin and pointed, which today was dripping unattractively. He was attired in a tunic of fine wool, belted at the waist with a cordoban leather belt over which was a sheepskin jerkin. Dark coloured hose were pushed into high boots, also of cordoban leather. His thin spindly legs and rather protuberant knees made him look sickly, but in reality he was sinewy and stronger than he appeared. The tithing men were eying him warily. This bailiff was renowned for his tetchy disposition and his unwillingness to act decisively unless it suited him. It did not suit him now, but he was he realised, being watched from afar by Sir Tobias, who could over rule him. He did not want that humiliation, so he had called the local tithing men together.

"Someone must know of a devil worshipping coven in our town," he growled.

"I want each of you to question all men in your tithing. There have been happenings in the forest, in the village of Motcombe and now in Enmore Green. Some of these have happened in broad daylight. The last one was at night. There is often fire involved and brutal cuts to the upper body. One of our number is as we speak seriously ill in the Abbey, having survived the attack on her husband."

The weather had changed, and as market traders stood together sheltering from the rain which drenched them and made trading unprofitable, they watched the bailiff oversee the fastening of two men in the stocks which were in the market place. They had been caught watering ale with urine from their horses,- brothers who traded from a small ale house on Bleke Street. One such trader, a fletcher, covered his quills with sacking to keep them dry and attempted a repair for a customer. Men were still required to practice archery at the town's butts, near the ancient castle, so there was still work , but the weather today was not promising.

They surveyed the scene gloomily. Water carriers toiling with a donkey laden with rough leather buckets disappeared into the cellars beneath St. Peter's church to deliver their load. Shaftesbury was not blessed with a good water supply. There was an ancient agreement with Gillingham, in whose manor the springs of Enmore Green lay, that water would be carried from the springs up to Shaftesbury daily. It was needed for many purposes, one of the important ones being the brewing of beer in the plentiful inns around the hill top town. St Peter's ale was brewed under the church, and the church itself was being partly rebuilt. It was a riot of colour inside, candles and lamps burning in front of the many chantry niches, and statues of saints and bishops, all gloriously gilded. The rushes on the earthen floor were always clean and sweet smelling, a credit to their priest and all who worshipped there.

The bailiff left his rooms and wandered indecisively outside, drips of rain falling on him as he slouched into the market. He scowled at the traders nearest to him as he made for the ale house at the bottom of Gold Hill. There were several there, but he favoured one in particular and met there with his friends, but today he was alone. His problem was one of divided friendships and uneasy thoughts concerning those in his circle. Where had the coroner been that it took him so long to get to the death house when the nun was killed? Why was his son not available for scribing when he was needed? How many more times would he have to excuse the coroner's drinking habits? He kicked at a stray dog which had wandered into the ale house as he left, resolutely putting aside his vague suspicions but too idle to address them lest it rebound on himself. He had too many secrets to hide to accuse anyone else.

Sherborne

Matthias realised he had forgotten to tell Martin the good news from Daniel de Thame...how he would be pleased for Martin to fashion a new shop sign for him.

He sought Martin at the end of his day; it had been a sad day for Matthias; there was no visit from Sir Tobias which boded ill for Matthias' proposition for Lady Alice. He was afraid he had stepped too close to be courteous causing Sir Tobias offence. He would be sorry if he lost his friendship. It had been on his mind all day, producing a heavy sinking feeling.

Martin was enjoying the evening air outside the barn, wearing his new leg and every now and then exerting pressure on it to give him the sensation of weight bearing.

"Do you think Master Jacobson will call soon, now he has returned from Shaftesbury?"

"You are eager to try walking, Martin! Take it slowly...but yes, I am certain he will not forget, and I have good news for you. Master de Thame, Daniel's father, would like you to make him a new shop sign. That's your first order.....if he is pleased maybe there will be more work to follow from others. Lydia will be pleased you have your first order."

Martin looked up quickly. "Do you think so? She was the first person who helped me when I was at my very lowest – apart from Sir Tobias and his family. Lydia has become a good friend to me."

"No more than a friend?" Matthias teased gently.

Martin coloured hotly. He frowned.

"Matthias. Look at me, - I am blind in one eye, scarred and have an amputated limb. I have no home of my own, no prospects apart from the hope that my skill with wood will bear fruit.....what can I possibly offer to any woman?"

"Warmth, companionship, love, affection, friend-ship." As he spoke Matthias remembered with regret that these were qualities that he would seek in a wife, and which had been no part of the conversation he'd had with Alice.

"Added to that," he continued with a flash of male humour, "There are still other more vital parts of you which work perfectly well."

Martin smiled in spite of himself, and the conversation turned to details of how he should begin the work for Daniel de Thame, but Matthias' words stayed in Martin's mind and gave him reason for hope.

Shaftesbury

Winifrith was restless in the Abbey. The novitiates were divided roughly into two parts, - those who had a true vocation and those who had been placed there by their parents for other reasons. One or two of those were very young, as young as nine or ten years, and Winifrith did not bother herself with them. The others were more interesting – and more daring. They had learned that they could leave the Abbey at certain times by a small gate leading on to Bimport, by Trinity church. It was just a bit of fun, Winifrith told herself, forgetful already of Imogen's fate.

The three novitiates enjoyed their walk to the marketplace, Winifrith in particular revelling in her ability and enjoyment at being free to swing her hips and swirl her skirt, quite a feat in a young nun. She was sinfully aware of admiring glances from her companions who were more modest in their walk, and wished for the company of young men, whom she knew she could attract. Although they were aiming to go to the market place, they knew they were unable to purchase goods, having no access to coin. No matter – they would enjoy the feeling of freedom for a short hour.

Two young men slouched on the barrels near The Swan hostelry. Winifrith eyed them boldly as she passed by. One of them winked at her and she giggled slightly.

The landlord of the Swan emerged from the door, frowning at the two men.

"Be off with you, young wastrels….you should be at your work…what call do you have to be so free with your looks? Those young ladies don't fool me…they look to be from the Abbey."

John Croxhale was an astute and upright citizen, owning the Swan hostelry and doing excellent trade. He had no time for such as the young who wasted good working time and dallied with unprotected girls – girls who in his opinion should not be out on the streets. He called to his wife inside the hostelry, and set off towards Gold Hill where the three were heading, now tailed by the two young men.

The walls of the Abbey were on one side of the market, thick, buttressed and tall. This wall marked the boundary of the Abbey grounds although much more of Shaftesbury and the surrounding area was owned by the Abbey. The market itself spread out down the steep hill towards the settlement at the bottom, called St. James. There were some handsome houses bordering the market on the opposite side of the Abbey wall, and at the top, the stocks, today containing two pedlars , fastened there for the day for selling false relics and annoying the pilgrims to the Abbey. Winifrith was pleased to be among the bustle and vibrancy of the place. The sounds of street sellers calling, the noise of children screaming and laughing as they dodged through the crowds, the smells of humanity, some pleasant, some not so – colours, noise, warmth, all excited her senses - what pretty ribbons there were on this stall. She paused, and without thinking twice, slipped a length of ribbon into her pocket. Her two companions had moved on, and Winifrith's heart dropped as she felt the heavy hand of the inn keeper on her shoulder.

John Croxhale glared at her and she dropped her eyes.

"You have come from the Abbey. This is not your rightful place," he told her.

"We are permitted to come out sometimes," Winifrith began, but he cut her off.

"You need to go back and do penance for the sin of theft….and for the sin of seeking the eyes of young men."

Winifrith sighed. "You sound just like my father."

"And where does he live?"

"Sherborne. I would like to be home again."

"Go back to the Abbey. Your father will have good reasons for your being there."

He watched her as she retraced her steps towards the High Street and thence to Bimport. Concerned by the recent deaths, he continued watching until he saw her two companions also return.

Master Coxhale was an upright citizen of Shaftesbury. He kept a healthy establishment, had daughters of his own and was concerned that a young maid should be able to leave the Abbey and walk in the town undetected by the mistress of novitiates, especially when there were evil doers in the area.

He was aware that some of the so called godly ladies enjoyed the company of men, and drank ale with them to excess in the Broad Hall near his establishment. He hoped the young women he had seen that day would be safe.

Winifrith was not intending to return to her place in the Abbey, however. She walked resolutely past the gate from which she had emerged; holding her head high, she strode past the main gate of the Abbey, unseen by the gatekeeper nun, and shedding her coif and veil, descended the steep track towards St. James. She thought longingly of the pretty ribbons she had to replace, and wished she had not been seen taking them... she would have so loved to wear them in her hair.

Spring was in the air. The track was well wooded here and as she descended, her light shoes became soiled with the heavy earth underfoot. She caught her habit on twigs showing green shoots of life, and turning to disentangle herself, she realised she had been followed by the young men at whom she had winked outside the Swan.

They did not appear so attractive to her now, alone at the bottom of this hill, but not yet within sight of dwelling places. Her heart beat faster as they approached her, sliding down the muddy track towards her. She was unprepared for what happened next; she stood no chance of escape as they threw a thick cloth over her head, pulling it tight around her neck before bundling her unceremoniously through the trees, half carrying her between them. She could smell horse dung on the cloth... and some other smell which she could not identify....it clogged her senses and she tried not to breathe. She was flung into a hollow in the damp undergrowth and to her horror she felt hands press against her mouth. She tried to bite at them, but this merely served to help them in their efforts to force the cloth into her mouth. More frightening than anything was the fact that they had not uttered a single word. She could hear their breath, panting with exertion as she fought back, but she was no match for two strong young men, fired with their own power over her.

In a surprisingly short time she felt her limbs lose their feeling, her mouth grow slack and a sick feeling overcame her before she lost consciousness.

Sherborne

Matthias opened his school two days after his interview with Sir Tobias with an increasingly heavy heart. It would appear that his offer to Alice had not been met with acceptance. He began the day with a logic exercise, designed to encourage reasonable and organized thinking. His attention wandered too frequently; he was aware of the boys becoming restless and knew it was due to his own mood. This would not do; he must lift himself out of this ....he supposed it meant he cared for Alice more than he realised. If Sir Tobias forced her into a marriage alliance against her will, how would she cope? But then, he mused, women were schooled to obey, mostly. What he had offered Alice was a way to disobey.

The restlessness of the scholars broke into his thoughts. They had all risen to their feet. He looked up, - Sir Tobias had entered with Lady Alice and was waiting quietly in front of the door for Matthias to acknowledge them. Matthias stood up awkwardly.

"Good Morning, Sir Tobias..Lady Alice. "

"Good Morning Master Barton. I believe we may have a business matter to discuss. Is Martin available to take your place for half an hour?"

Matthias sent one of the boys to fetch Martin, who was working on his commission for Daniel de Thame.

"I would like Lady Alice to accompany us and be party to our discussion," the Coroner stated. Matthias ushered them into his own room leading off the schoolroom and closed the door firmly, leaving Martin to continue with an exercise in copying.

Matthias felt distinctly nervous, dry mouth, tight chest, clenched hands. Lady Alice seemed calm, although subdued; she did not meet his eyes.

Sir Tobias sat himself in the one chair, leaving Lady Alice and Matthias standing; Matthias felt like a naughty schoolboy waiting to be reprimanded.

"So you have made my daughter an offer of a partnership in your school, Matthias?"

Matthias relaxed a little. This was more friendly than using his Master Barton handle.

"I believe Lady Alice would be an asset to the growth of the school, Sir. She has a good rapport with the scholars and is a patient and thorough teacher."

"What security are you able to offer her, Matthias?"

Matthias was floored for a moment or two. He thought furiously. Security? Did he mean financial? Was he meaning the necessity of a contract in case the school floundered? Was he expected to offer half his house as security?

"I had not considered that aspect, Sir Tobias." It seemed to Matthias that honesty was the best path.

"I thought not. It was a kindly offer, Matthias, but made in haste, I think. Yesterday I took Lady Alice to Poyntington to meet with Sir Stephen, who is seeking a wife, following the death some years ago of his lady. We went merely as guests for dinner. I wanted Alice to see the house of which she would be mistress if I took the matter further. His sisters also live there. My wife accompanied us to what was a pleasant, if sedentary dinner. Lady Alice has expressed a wish to remain a widow for the moment to explore the offer you have made her. I have to consider how taking this offer will affect her. It will negate the possibility of an alliance at Poyntington – Sir Stephen will have other ladies in mind – and will prevent my seeking any other alliances for the moment. You yourself have, I believe, some private means, and the school is gathering momentum with good reports of progress. In what way can we establish Lady Alice as an equal partner, - if indeed that is what you intend?"

Matthias paused to bring a stool forward from the corner for Lady Alice to be seated before turning his mind to some kind of plan.

"I have always been honest with you, Sir Tobias. My offer was entirely spontaneous, made on the spur of the moment, but very genuinely made. I have enjoyed working with Lady Alice. I have been impressed by her natural ability to impart learning, and as we are expanding slowly, it would be a huge advantage to have a second person with the same goals as my own. I have not considered any financial implications, but that can be discussed in more detail."

Alice, from her silent seat in the corner of the room, felt invisible. She had not thought they would be discussing her so dispassionately. In truth, she was longing for Matthias to break, to crack his outward serene, courteous demeanour and to offer warmth, companionship, humour.....where had she gone wrong in her appeal to him?

When they had worked over Martin in the barn on the frightening night he had been so badly injured by the soldier Rafe, she had experienced a comfortable sensation of companionship as they fought together to stem the bleeding and keep Martin alive.

Why had that not blossomed? What had made Matthias retreat from her? She felt she had miscalculated. She had tried so hard ....perhaps too hard.

She heard her father's deal with Matthias and tried to feel excitement.

"Let us try this arrangement for six months, Matthias. During that time, Alice will be your assistant in the school, with no financial ties or obligation to make any suggestions or decisions. If at the end of that time you wish to make her an equal partner in the business sense, and Alice still wishes to pursue that course, then we will draw up a suitable agreement."

"That is a generous suggestion, Sir Tobias. Thank you. Lady Alice, I look forward to working with you on a more frequent basis."

So formal...so cold...she had thought there might be more. She stood up.

"Thank you Father. Thank you Matthias. I will start straight away so that we might form a suitable arrangement."

Very factual....very unemotional...he thought she might have been more enthusiastic.

He hoped he had not made a mistake but the arrangement was made, there was no going back. He would be working with Alice from now on.

Towards Sherborne

Brother John continued his wearisome journey. He had no option now. His heart was giving frequent and troublesome flutters; he was tired, dispirited, broken hearted at the destruction of his chosen place of retreat. His destination was Ilchester, his mother house, but first he would go to Sherborne. There was something he would like to see once more before he went to his maker.

He had sheltered the first night at the friary in nearby Gillingham. The infirmarian had tried to persuade him to remain a little longer to rest, but he was anxious to press on and reach his destination before it was too late.

He was unable to cover much ground each day,- he had been travelling for five days now, mostly on foot, and had rested from time to time in the priest's house of churches along the way...usually a welcome, a frugal meal and an opportunity to celebrate mass. Now he was near to West Stour, faltering in his steps today with stiffness in his joints which almost amounted to pain.

A dishevelled young girl approached him as he rested by the side of the track. She was limping, her underskirt was bloodied, her feet bare. There was a discoloured bruise on her face and her eyes were half closed.

"Where are you bound?" she faltered.

"First, to Sherborne, then onwards to Ilchester," replied the friar.

"I beg you, let me walk with you…"

"You have been in trouble?"

"I have been much abused…violated…suffocated. I am not certain how anything happened…I only remember the cloth thrown over my face.…it had a strong smell which sickened me…when I woke I was alone…my habit was gone..my shoes.…"

"Your habit? You are a nun?"

"I was…am… a novitiate at Shaftesbury.…I am trying to go home.…I cannot conform to the rule. There were two men…" She stopped, panic suddenly overcame her as she spoke, remembering the fate of Imogen on her last attempt to return home.

"Was there fire? Masks?" Brother John asked her urgently, but Winifrith shook her head.

"There wasn't the same feeling as before."

"Before? This has happened to you before?"

Winifrith told him of the previous incident when she and Imogen had tried to return to their homes, and of the appearance of the men, masked and screaming. There was none of this – she felt these were different men, intent only on violation. Strangely. she had no real sense of danger, no mourning for Imogen, no lingering nightmare of that occassion. A strangely detached young woman was Winifrith…slightly simple.…… vaguely promiscuous.…..an innocent accident waiting to happen.

But even so she could not tell him of her soreness, of the pain which caused her to limp badly, the searing ache in her loins, bruised and bleeding. She recognized this friar as a pillar of goodness as physically frail as she was mentally frail.

This strange ill assorted pair travelled on together.

Shaftesbury

Sister Gratiana was the infirmarian of the Abbey; she kept an orderly pharmacy, a strict rule of calm, a firm hand on her patients. She had watched carefully over Jenna, waiting to administer mandragora for pain relief as soon as she showed signs of waking. Her shoulder wound was now clean despite its depth. It was bound with clean soft wool infused with herbs and honey, the great healer. She was now breathing with a regular pattern, and Sister Gratiana was sure she would rouse soon. It was now nearly three weeks since she had been found by Brother John.

The infirmary was well away from the busiest part of the great Abbey, - slightly to the left of the kitchens, and enjoying views from the graceful windows over the escarpment towards the South, overlooking the little settlement of St. James.

Her young helper, Sister Agnes, was detailed to watch over Jenna on this day, allowing Sister Gratiana time to observe the offices of the day, pray and read her book of hours. Sister Agnes had sat silently by the cot watching Jenna, noticing the faded bruises and the more relaxed breathing. She had been working with Sister Gratiana for more than a year now, and although she enjoyed the work, she did not have Sister Gratiana's instinctive feel for the welfare of the patients. She looked longingly through the curved windows at the early Spring sunshine and longed to feel the sun on her face. She glanced at

Jenna....no, no change...still sleeping. She would go outside just for a few moments, - no harm in that.

Because she was outside, she was not there to observe Jenna's first terrified waking moments. Because she was outside, she was not there to prevent the man who had slipped past the gate keeper to attempt to see the one who had lived. Because she was outside, she was not there to help Jenna in her strangled scream.....It was Sister Gratiana who had returned to retrieve a forgotten item who chanced upon the man as he tightened his grip round Jenna's throat. She was a strong woman and did not hesitate. He was so absorbed in his intended action – squeezing hard on Jenna's throat with his thumbs – that he had not heard Sister Gratiana enter and was unprepared for her grip on his hair, jerking his head back hard, forcing him to release his hold. He whirled round, snarling with fury, spitting in Sister Gratiana's face. She, gasping with revulsion as spittle ran into her eyes and down her face, lost her grip on his hair, and so he was gone, leaving Jenna now awake but moaning, bruises already visible on each side of her throat.

Sister Gratiana cradled Jenna in her arms, calling for Sister Agnes. There would be penance for Sister Agnes, but first Jenna must be calmed, her new bruises attended to and then guarded even more closely.

News of Jenna's awakening reached Ezekiel the next day. Abbess Stourton sent a messenger, and Ezekiel prepared to leave for Shaftesbury at once. Martha would have liked to accompany him but wisely, Ezekiel decided to call on Sir Tobias for support. Sir Tobias was away from home, doing Coroner's business in Dorchester with the Bailiff. Lady Bridget felt uneasy allowing Ezekiel to return to Shaftesbury alone, so she suggested calling on Matthias' services. Despite the delay this caused, it was a sensible move, and now Matthias had Lady Alice as his assistant, it was easy to accomplish. Alice had slipped easily into her new role, awkwardness at first making life stilted, but as they were both keen to make the unusual arrangement work the smooth running of duties helped to dissipate the difficulty. She relished the chance to organize the remainder of the day and probably the following one, too. Martin was working in the barn, - she knew she could call on him if she needed his help.

Matthias and Ezekiel arrived in Shaftesbury in the late afternoon. Ezekiel went at once to the Abbey whilst Matthias sought lodgings for the night for them.

Sister Gratiana had soothed Jenna to sleep and it was arranged that a visit tomorrow would be more suitable. Ezekiel was able to look on his sister, sleeping now, with the bruises on her throat still visible. Abbess Stourton had summoned the bailiff to investigate the intrusion of the Abbey which could so easily have cost Jenna her life; she found him unsatisfactorily evasive and shifty.

"Sister Agnes is doing penance for her lack of attention," Sister Gratiana told him.

Matthias had found a room for them at the Swan, where they found their host, John Croxhale, congenial and talkative. His premises was clean, airy, one of the better ones in the town, situated on the High Street, and overlooking St. Peter's church. There were many ale houses and hostelries in Shaftesbury; it was a good stopping place for parties travelling from London to Exeter, there were several markets in the town attracting traders from the surrounding area and beyond and the pilgrims to the beautiful Abbey came from some distances and needed places to stay.

John Croxhale joined them during the evening for a jar of ale.

"I think I met a Sherborne girl, or rather I reprimanded one...a young novitiate from the Abbey."

Matthias groaned. "Not the Keylewey girl?"

"I forget the name...she was out in the market, helping herself to ribbons from a stall."

"I think the Keyleweys have much trouble with her. She is quite silly and possibly truly simple in her head. They have done the best they can for her."

"I followed her to make sure she returned to the Abbey – she had slipped out with two other young girls. I followed her until she reached the gate."

"That was good of you," Ezekiel commented.

"I have daughters of my own..and there were a couple of idle young men far too interested in them... I wanted to make sure she was safe."

Matthias recalled the shallow chatter and attempted flirting Winifrith had indulged in on the journey from Sherborne, and hoped she would stay safe in the Abbey this time.

Shaftesbury

Mistress Sarah Keylewey was preparing to assist Dame Margaret with the collection for the Almshouse when the steward from Shaftesbury Abbey knocked on her door. A flustered maid servant admitted him and Sarah's heart fell when she realised who had called.

"My husband is still away from home," she began, hoping this was no more than a complaint about

Winifrith's last escapade, but she was mistaken. The news was graver.

"I must tell you this news despite the absence of your husband," the steward told her, uncertainly. "Your daughter has disappeared from the Abbey....we have searched the surrounding area but it would appear she is making for home once more. Abbess Stourton would like to know as soon as she appears here....this is the second time she has absconded. The Abbess would like to consult with your husband when he returns. Will he be absent long?"

"Possibly a few more days. He has accompanied Master Rochell to London on business connected with the licence from his Grace the King for the new almshouse."

The steward left with the promise that Sarah Keylewey would send a messenger as soon as Winifrith arrived, but after he had left, Sarah fretted that the Abbess would not have their wayward daughter, despite the silver they had contributed towards the Abbey. She discussed her problems with Dame Margaret as they worked, calling on tenements, explaining the construction planned and collecting coin or in some cases, generous offers of rents from lands.

"You have not made a request to the Abbot?" Sarah asked, attempting to put her worry behind.

"I plan to," was the enigmatic reply, and I do not think I will be refused."

After the two women separated to divide up their work, Dame Margaret turned into Hound Street and tapped on the door of a small tenement. She was admitted without question. The inside of the tenement was dark but clean, the floor swept meticulously, fresh rushes smelled sweet and Mistress Amice looked comfortable with the young babe on her arm.

"How are you finding this?" Dame Margaret asked the young woman.

"I have loved every moment," Mistress Amice assured her. "Am I able to ask her parentage?"

"That must remain private, but I can assure you it is of Sherborne. Will you continue?"

"I will indeed. My husband says he has a need now to work hard for us."

Dame Margaret smiled to herself. She would attempt to see that a little extra coin came into this home on a regular basis. She went on her way, satisfied.

Later she called on the Abbot. It was with some difficulty that she managed to obtain a private interview, Prior William being insistent at first that he could deal with whatever the matter concerned. Possibly he was aware of the babe, but Dame Margaret needed to be sure. Gossip and rumour spread so quickly in enclosed societies as well as in small towns.

"Mistress Amice has had the babe for a week now," she told him, sitting in his comfortable house, admiring his glassed windows, the rich tapestries on the walls and the rugs underfoot. She had not been offered refreshment.

"Does she wish to make the arrangement permanent?" The Abbot tried hard to be more friendly than was his normal self when speaking to townspeople, particularly those who had been instrumental in the battle of the fonts....still not resolved. His anger and pride were still troubling his soul.

"I think she would be willing to make this a long term commitment, however, although clean and hard-working, this couple have little spare coin. The addition of a child is heavy on the purse."

The Abbot was silent, one hand stroking his chin in thought. He cleared his throat awkwardly.

"I believe we own the tenements in Hound Street."

Dame Margaret nodded. She was aware that the Abbey was landlord to many in the town.

"To reduce their rent would give some indication of possible parentage," mused Abbot Bradford.

Dame Margaret nodded sagely again. Inwardly she felt a glow of satisfaction, - she had the haughty Abbot just where she wanted him – and she had not finished with him yet!

"I could arrange for a monthly purse to be available to the family, anonymously, of course, through Sherborne bankers."

"That would be most acceptable, My Lord Abbot. And you will of course now wish to contribute to the fund for the building of the new almshouse?"

Abbot Bradford squirmed, inwardly. This woman had formidable cheek! He would have liked to refuse, but he felt it would be unwise.

He mentioned as small a sum as he could. Dear God – she hadn't finished yet!

"And possibly some timber from one of the Abbey holdings to aid the building? Stout oak wood is best so I believe."

"That can be arranged when you are ready to begin to build, Dame Margaret."

He signed his name against her list. The donation was made.

Shaftesbury

Ezekiel visited the Abbey at first light. He was keen to see how Jenna would be...she had been unconscious for three weeks and was now in danger as she lay there.

He was angry with the sister who had left her alone, but there seemed little point in remonstrating with Abbess Stourton. It was internal discipline and he must accept that. He did not want to endanger his chances of regular visits to Jenna, nor spoil the fragile chance of Jenna remembering vital details of her ordeal. He understood that she had reported the matter to the sullen bailiff. There was little more he could do.

Abbess Stourton had been most adamant that only Ezekiel would be admitted, so Matthias had to accept some time to explore the market town on his own. He thought he might speak further with John Croxhale or seek out the coroner and bailiff .

Ezekiel sat by the cot in the lime washed room where Jenna lay. She was awake, weak and seemed only dimly to recognize her brother. She was unable to name him although she accepted his careful embrace and showed no fear of him. He stroked her hand as he spoke quietly to her of Martha and the boys. He thought it best not to mention Isaac just yet for fear of causing greater distress than she was able to bear.

He was unsure that she had really understood who Martha was, merely nodding and smiling uncertainly. After half an hour he left, arranging with Sister Gratiana to return later in the day.

"She is not herself," he told Matthias sadly as they shared a simple meal .

"I did expect that, but it still comes as a shock. She is certainly not able to give us any help regarding her husband's killers."

"Let me go over the events carefully," Matthias suggested. "Perhaps some local knowledge might be an advantage," he added, as John Croxhale joined them with his ale. "Most of these events happened in Shaftesbury or its immediate surrounds, and some extra information might be helpful. I don't think the bailiff or the coroner here have made any progress. I could not find either of them this morning when I searched."

"They are not the most prodigious of fellows we have had in office," John Croxhale volunteered.

"Your coroner is much too fond of his drink, I believe," Matthias commented. He warmed to John Croxhale after their conversation of the previous evening. Maybe some more information might come of simple sharing of events.

"The first incident was the disappearance of Jenna and Isaac," he began. John Croxhale interrupted him.

"There have been a series of smaller events leading up to that, now I come to think of it," he said. "There have been reports of three or four mysterious fires in an isolated house over the last year, and some children came to report seeing men dancing naked over a fire... nothing was done as it was dismissed by most as a wild tale designed to shock, but a little while after that, a frightened maid was discovered hiding in a the same disused house, telling a story of seeing men with masks....that was dismissed too...it was said that the maid was simple and had enjoyed too much strong ale. She left the town soon after – no-one knew where she went."

"Did no-one think to follow these up?"

"They were all isolated incidents – I don't think anyone attached any significance to them....only now can I see that it is possible that they might all be connected."

"Jenna and Isaac seem to be the first violent happenings, unless the maid was harmed and disposed of..."

"The fires were down in the village of Motcombe... It was actually over a year ago....we heard about it a little while after the event when a group of villagers brought produce up to market. They were puzzled by the fires, as they thought a crippled man was living there at the time, but there was no sign of him afterwards. They thought he might have fired it by accident, trying to keep warm, but there was no sign of a body.....they enquired whether he had been seen in Shaftesbury."

"That has to be Martin Cooper," Matthias exclaimed. "He found his way to Sherborne, amazingly. He is an amputee from the King's wars in France....his mother lived in a village near Shaftesbury....she left with a tinker whilst he was in France. He lost the sight of one eye and his lower leg. He spoke recently of sheltering in his mother's old house and witnessing men chanting and burning fire....This ties up too well not to be true."

"You know him?" asked Master Croxhale in surprise.

"He is lodging in my barn at present," Matthias told him. "He has quite a history....he is no beggar. He was squire to a knight fighting in France and was badly wounded, and then wounded some more last year when a fellow soldier caught up with him....Master Jacobson here was the surgeon who saved his life....that is how we became acquainted."

"An astonishing tale!"

"Maybe Isaac was not the first death," Ezekiel suggested, thinking of the maid who had disappeared.

"No reports of a body have been made," John Croxhale commented.

"She may have simply returned to her home....but no-one has made any enquiries about her. It is possible that she was alone with no relatives to ask."

"Jenna would have died too if Brother John had not found her."

Matthias explained the ruined chapel in the forest...a forest which was now so overgrown in parts that it had become a haven for wolfheads, poachers and returning soldiers if they cared to fight their way through the thick undergrowth. It had also proved a haven for the isolated friar, hoping to live out his days in solitude and prayer.

"The foresters keep part of the area in good hunting condition, but it is a large area and the verderers and foresters have left parts of it to grow wild. It was once a hunting forest for King John many years ago. The lodge is now ruined."

"So Isaac was the first death about which we knew... and but for the intervention of Brother John, Jenna could well have been the second."

"The next incident was the young novitiate from the Abbey.....in day light and taken from a fairly well used track, as I recall. Then she was dragged towards the forest for what? A ritual death? To be a plaything?"

"The third," Matthias continued, as John Croxhale rose to replenish their ale, "was the midwife from Enmore Green....in darkness. Very near to her own home, too."

"The wounds on all were very similar," observed Ezekiel. "The shoulders or chests had been slashed...an attempt to reach the heart, maybe?" He shuddered. His work as a barber surgeon had seen many desecrations of human flesh, but most were caused by accident or war. This was wilful desecration for evil purposes.

"Whoever these people are, it would appear their sense of the use of the knife is inaccurate, their knowledge of the anatomy of the body is rather wild. The wounds we have seen are ragged and must have been made in haste, hoping they would find their mark."

"These fires are significant," Ezekiel noted, frowning into his ale. He was becoming impatient to return to the Abbey to visit Jenna again, but he curbed his impatience.

Matthias sighed. He thought he should probably return to Sherborne and leave Ezekiel here for a few days, but the temptation to try and see Jenna if she roused a little was huge.

A second visit to the Abbey Infirmary proved more successful. Matthias accompanied Ezekiel, and to their surprise, Sister Gratiana allowed Matthias in.

Jenna was still weak but was washed and awake, lying submissively against the white pillow.

"I think you are my brother Ezekiel," she whispered. Ezekiel's face crumpled with emotion. He drew his hands over his eyes and managed a smile as he knelt by the simple cot.

Matthias squatted on the floor with his back to the wall. He did not want to alarm Jenna in any way.

"Do you remember what happened to you, Jenna?"

Jenna frowned.....turned her head away from him. There was silence. After a pause, she murmured, "There was a fight in the kitchen......I can't remember why..... he hurt my arms...." Her eyes closed. "I can't remember...I can't talk about it."

Matthias wandered outside to gaze at the view from the top. The original hill town of Shaftesbury had been well chosen by their ancestors...one could see for miles here, - he could view the rolling verdant countryside spread out before him as far as his eye could see. In the past, watchful eyes from this point would see anything which moved long before danger became imminent.

Ezekiel joined him after a short while. Jenna had refused to tell him any more, - if indeed she remembered anything of value,- and had fallen asleep again.

The two men walked through the Abbey quietly, emerging into the courtyard which was busy, contrasting sharply with the silence inside the Abbey, once they were clear of the waiting pilgrims. As they passed the novitiate's doorway, Matthias thought of Winifrith and wondered whether she had settled down here after her last escapade. It would seem not after the conversation with John Croxhale.

They were just about to go through the Abbey Gateway which led on to Bimport when the Mistress of Novitiates, whom they had met briefly when they had returned Winifrith recently, scurried after them, touching Matthias on the sleeve to attract his attention.

"Forgive me for intruding on your conversation... I recognize you, sir, as the person who returned Winifrith from her home.....she has absconded yet again.....I have hesitated to tell Abbess Stourton.....she will think me lax in my supervision....I have tried to be strict with her but she is very wilful and ignorant of the dangers ..."

"When did you last see her? Matthias asked her, concerned at this news. It did not look well for the Keyleweys, who were trying to do their best for this wayward daughter.

"Two days ago...she took herself into the town with others against my wishes. They returned, but Winifrith did not."

"I plan to return to Milborne Port today, but I can ride on to Sherborne to see if she has returned home again," Matthias told her. "But you should inform Abbess Stourton. This could be serious, although I pray it is just Winifrith returning home once more."

They moved out onto Bimport and strode back to the Swan to collect their horses from John Croxhale, who had proved a congenial host. He was aghast at the news that Winifrith had not returned to the Abbey. He regretted turning back as he saw her draw level with the gate, but the deed was done. He remembered the two young men who had flirted so openly with her... he felt sure he knew them but could not place them. He agreed to look out for the two men to question them, and to watch for any suggestion of Winifrith found on track ways around. Ezekiel now wished to return to the Abbey, and Matthias decided to return home, keeping his eyes open for a sighting of Winifrith. He knew he would have to see the Keyleweys if he did not find her on the road.

Sherborne

Brother John and Winifrith made slow progress. Winifrith was unaware of the grey pallor of Brother John's face and laboured breathing; she had problems of her own, aching loins and bloodied thighs made walking painful. She was not a person given to considering the feelings of others, looking only to herself, and this journey was agony for both of them. The friar tried to pray as he stumbled onwards, watching the novice carefully for he was moved by her weakened condition and could only guess at the details of her recent experience. They took shelter on the fourth night in the church at Henstridge, needing to rest well into the morning before joining the track again, which is how Matthias came to miss them altogether as he rode towards Sherborne

Sarah Keylewey was immediately anxious when Matthias called, fearing the worst in view of Imogen's fate. Winifrith was not, of course at home, but neither was her father, being still away in London on business for the licence of the almshouse.

Leaving Mistress Keylewey to call in favours from her own friends and neighbours, Matthias went straight to Purse Caundle to speak with Sir Tobias.

Sir Tobias felt the gravity of the situation immediately. He was afraid that Winifrith had fallen as the next victim of the coven.

He wondered how to put all these fragments of information together....it seemed especially hard since the problems were so far away....Shaftesbury had their own officers yet they did not appear to be too troubled by the unsolved deaths and sinister coven. If Winifrith had met with a similar fate, then the affair certainly did touch Sherborne as well. Sir Tobias and William mounted and set out towards Shaftesbury, leaving Matthias to return to his own home.

They rode carefully along the trackway leading to Shaftesbury. Wherever there were thickets, they stopped, dismounted and beat the undergrowth, calling for the girl. They found nothing. They continued towards Henstridge; Sir Tobias realised that any search Mistress Keylewey had managed to organize would have started from Sherborne, so they would be behind him. He planned to go as far as Shaftesbury if necessary and start looking in the surrounding area of the Abbey. This was an unpleasant affair, and one in which he had felt unable to be too directly involved. Perhaps he should now call on his office and be more direct with the bailiff in Shaftesbury.

They had reached the half way point between Milborne Port and Henstridge when William stood up in his stirrups and directed his gaze to what appeared to be a bundle of cloth propped against a tree a little way off the track. The bundle moved and a hand attempted a wave. William dismounted, hobbled his mount and Sir Tobias followed suit. The friar was lying weakly against the bole of a tree, his robes travel stained and torn. He looked up at Sir Tobias through eyes clouded with pain.

"The young novitiate has gone to find me some water.." he rasped, hoarsely.

His head drooped down on his chest as the next spasm of pain gripped him. William knelt to hold him when he shuddered to breathe again as the pain receded.

Winifrith staggered across the rough ground, close to exhaustion herself, but with her underskirt deliberately soaked in pond water.

"Brother, use my underskirt to bathe your head... there was nothing to carry the water...I found a pond... but do not drink...it is dirty..."

For once in her life, Winifrith showed concern for this fellow traveller of hers. She appeared not to notice the Coroner and his squire, so exhausted was she. She knelt on the rough ground and tenderly bathed the friar's head and hands.

Sir Tobias crouched beside her. He took her torn and bleeding hands in his.

"Winifrith...what has happened to you? Who is this friar?"

Winifrith gazed at him as though she was seeing him for the first time, suddenly aware of his presence. She looked in bewilderment at both men.

"I don't know.....he found me walking....I found him walking.....we have walked together. Now he needs more help than I....and I have no strength to go on..."

William lifted Brother John in his arms and carried him to his horse. Sir Tobias supported Winifrith across to his own horse. As he lifted her he became aware of the pain such movement caused her; she winced as her body met the saddle and a small cry of distress escaped her. Sir Tobias noticed the blood on her shift and understood that she was only part clothed.

"You have been violated?"

She nodded, tears sliding down her cheeks.

William needed help with Brother John. The pains wracked him every few minutes, and William needed to mount first and Brother John was then lifted gently in front of him where William hoped he had strength enough to hold on to the high saddle horn.

It was a slow journey back to Sherborne. They met the posse searching for Winifrith on their outward journey who turned to follow, sending word ahead of them to the Abbey that the infirmarian would be needed, for although Sir Tobias recognized that Brother John was not of their order, the monks at Sherborne would be able to provide assistance for him.

He was uncertain what he should do for Winifrith, but Sarah Keylewey helped her daughter from his mount and together with a neighbour disappeared into her house, whilst William rode on to the Abbey with the friar.

Brother John seemed dazed and unaware of where he was. Two brothers took charge and helped him into their infirmary and William waited for Sir Tobias before they sought audience with Abbot Bradford.

Sir Tobias related the finding of the friar and the missing novitiate; Abbot Bradford frowned.

"How did they come to be thus together?"

"I am as wise as you, My Lord Abbot. When he has recovered a little, you must ask him. He is unknown to me."

"...and the girl? Is she really a novitiate? From Shaftesbury, I presume?"

"Yes, she really is, although I'm afraid a recalcitrant one. She is the daughter of William Keylewey. She has been placed at Shaftesbury but to my certain knowledge has absconded twice. I can tell you that when I found her, she was administering to this ailing brother, but she hardly realised our presence; I fear she has been cruelly violated."

Abbot Bradford's face, normally haughty, blanched visibly.

"I have some work to do with this Dominican," he said, sternly.

Sir Tobias held up a warning hand. "Softly softly, Father Abbot...I suspect he is a dying man, and what you suspect may be inaccurate. He is an old man, frail and sick."

"I intend to find out, never the less."

Sir Tobias left him, hoping the Abbot would not perform as his usual self.

Sherborne

What suddenly seemed a tale of two Abbeys now needed unravelling. Matthias suggested that he should return to Shaftesbury. Ezekiel had not yet returned home, so Matthias visited Martha before he left to invite the two boys to join the scholars until Ezekiel returned. He left the following day, leaving Sir Tobias to seek details of Winifrith's ordeal from her, and to visit Abbot Bradford to ascertain whether any more information could be gleaned from the sick friar.

Ezekiel was pleased to receive news of his family from Matthias when they met in The Swan. Ezekiel had visited Jenna daily; her recovery was slow and the nuns were now very watchful of visitors, but no further attempt had been made to see her by unknown persons.

Matthias took some time to recount new information to Ezekiel who was unaware of the finding of Winifrith and Brother John.

"What a tangle of monstrous events," Ezekiel sighed. John Croxhale joined them, over hearing the news concerning Winifrith.

"I moved a couple of young men on who were harassing the girls…although they did appear to enjoy being harassed. One of them is the son of the local coroner I think, - I knew I had seen him before.. I watched one girl, it must have been the one you call Winifrith, until she reached the Abbey gate. Sadly I thought she would turn in…apparently she did not. She must have continued down the hill…the ground is quite rough there with much vegetation and scrub…. I don't think the young men were following her, but they may have done so at a distance."

"Our friend the inebriated coroner…" said Matthias, thoughtfully. He recalled the first time they had met him…barely able to stand, soft buskins on his feet instead of working boots….truculent…and then John Croxhale's impression of him as an incompetent official.

"Clearly he does not have much control over his son. Is the young man idle, or is he apprenticed to a trade?"

"He is clerk to his father. I'm not quite sure how we came to have such a bunch of slapdash officials. We have two members of parliament representing Shaftesbury – we rarely see them….we should have two coroners but currently we have only one…the bailiff likes to be seen to be popular with the less ruly factions in the town…" John Croxhale tailed off, embarrassed at the state of things in his home town.

"How connected to the Abbey is the town?"

"Very connected…The Abbess is entitled to call on able bodied men to fight for the King…many businesses are reliant on the Abbey for trade…..like most great religious houses, the Abbey owns farms, mills, bakehouses…..without the Abbey Shaftesbury would be a poorer place altogether."

"Is the Abbess good and fair?"

"Abbess Stourton is a local lady of some worth. She has pulled the Abbey back from some wild behaviours in the recent past under the previous Abbess, but it is not perfect. There are still reports of lax rules….but far fewer than before….Abbess Stourton has imposed order but she is also very good at covering up misdeeds.

"What sort of misdeeds?" Matthias wondered.

"Chiefly drunkenness, partying inappropriately…. some of the novitiates find the rule too hard to follow and walk out in the town seeking lighthearted amusement...that is why your Winifrith walked in the town. Because of the pilgrims visiting the Abbey there are always strangers in the town who bring colour and variety to our life – and much trade, too. Yes, we would certainly miss the Abbey."

Matthias thought of what he knew of Sherborne Abbey – not as rich as Shaftesbury, but offering much employment for the townspeople...Sherborne would also miss its Abbey despite the dominant ownership of much of the town.

"How long ago was it that Shaftesbury had a Jewish community?" The thought came to Matthias quite suddenly.

"Many many years, I would say," the taverner told him, "it was nearly one hundred and sixty years ago when King Edward expelled all Jews from England. Why do you ask? What has this to do with anything?"

Ezekiel took a decision.

"Our family converted to Christianity in 1282, living in the Domus Conversorum. I think my ancestors must have forseen the coming expulsion and decided to adopt the Christian faith. It is long ago...we are fully committed to the blessed Eucharist and the Holy Catholic church. I have no idea why or how whoever did this to my sister and her husband could possibly know this. Perhaps it was because they looked slightly Jewish facially.... perhaps because they chose not to join in with some activities....my sister has always been quite shy, not wishing to dance or engage in gossip...." John Croxhale held up his hand, stopping Ezekiel in mid sentence.

"Stop! You do not need to justify your family.... I know Jenna and Isaac....they have been members of our community for some years. I think you are right when you mentioned facial appearance....there is nothing else at all that indicates a difference."

"So is this just co-incidence that they were targeted?" Matthias wondered, frowning at the complexity of the muddle.

"The next victim was a young nun. From what Winifrith told us, she was simply plucked from the path as they walked....that doesn't seem to follow any pattern, nor the next one.....although the first two were during daylight and Annestese was murdered during the hours of darkness. I'm not so sure that Winifrith's experience is quite the same...I need to hear what Sir Tobias has discovered."

"Strangely," Ezekiel mused, "both the first and the second times there were two people but only one was taken...the second was apparently discarded. That makes me wonder whether these incidents are fuelled by hallucinatory substances. In such cases the effects of the substances can induce a type of hysteria and confusion...and the slashes are indicative of an attempt at exposing the heart but missed due to lack of experience, knowledge or simply haste brought about by whatever substance is used."

"But where would such substances be obtained?" the taverner questioned. There was a reliable apothecary in the town, but no back street hags plying their trade, well, certainly not in this town. He had lived in Shaftsbury all his life, - he did not want to think of it as a place where evil could be purchased.

"Don't forget there are pilgrims who come regularly from all around, sometimes even further. Do any of them visit regularly, maybe to do illicit trade in such substances?"

"I suppose it is possible."

Matthias was frustrated. He had hoped to gain some clarity but they seemed to be going round in futile circles. He did not feel he could spend too much more time on this.- Shaftesbury had officials who could and should be investigating this themselves.

It was not even Sir Tobias' case....he had tried to keep his distance.

"Where might I find the young men who followed the young nuns?" he asked, unsure of how he would be able to approach them. John Croxhale gave him directions to the house of the local coroner, where his son, the clerk, could be found.

Matthias tried, but only a serving wench was there, telling him that the clerk had gone away. Deeply suspicious, Matthias left Cann and returned to the Abbey to find Ezekiel.

Sherborne

Abbot Bradford was mindful of the Coroner's words as he approached the infirmary where Brother Francis was caring for the weakened friar. However, he must discover whether this Brother had defiled the young nun. He was mindful of his recent need to find a place for a baby which spoke eloquently of the declining standards in religious houses and told much about the insatiable needs of some men. He had dealt with that swiftly and with severity, knowing the culprit. He must deal with his Dominican visitor gently but insistently.

Brother Francis was moving quietly about the room in which the friar had been housed. He was skilled in healing and had administered small amounts of digitalis to Brother John, who was in less pain now, and awake, though drowsy.

"Leave us please, Brother Francis."

"Be still in your talking, My Lord Abbot. He is very frail."

The Abbot inclined his head. He did not like being told what to do by one of his monks, but he acknowledged the advice and determined to abide by it.

He sat down by the cot, making the sign of the cross over Brother John.

"Bendicte, Brother."

"Benedicte, Father Abbot." The voice was weak, the eyes half closed, the mouth compressed with poorly concealed pain.

"My son, I have to ask you how you met the novitiate Winifrith. What is she to you?"

"Father Abbot, I know not who she is." He willed his heart to cease its painful flutter, making speech and thought difficult, despite the digitalis which had eased it a little.

"How did she come by her state of disarray?"

Brother John was silent, trying to gather his thoughts together. She had approached him on the path, distressed, bloodied and clearly in great discomfort. He had not asked her any questions regarding her state just glad to be able to help her by agreeing to allow her to walk with him. She had assisted him when he had collapsed and tried to fetch water....the rest he could not remember.

He tried, in halting sentences to convey this information to the Abbot, who listened, resolving to seek out Mistress Keylewey to verify the account against Winifrith's own, which he was sure she would have given to her mother.

"Father Abbot, it is my desire to return to Ilchester, my mother house. I have come to Sherborne to see ....." he broke off, mid sentence, wracked with pain which prevented him from speaking. Abbot Bradford summoned Brother Francis in haste, who held him in his arms, weak wine moistening his lips. By the time the spasm had passed, the Abbot had left, promising to return later. He was not good with visible suffering.

Mistress Keylewey received Abbot Bradford coolly, wary of his purpose in calling on her unannounced. Her husband was still away with Richard Rochell. The almshouse business took much time.

"My purpose is to question your daughter, Mistress....There are unanswered questions regarding the friar who accompanied her." The Abbot managed to make himself look stern and unbending – without too much effort, it has to be said.

"My daughter is resting, My Lord Abbot. What is it you wish to k now?"

"The very nature of their relationship, Mistress..." he faltered suddenly, uncertain how to frame the question.

"Winifrith has ever been a trouble to us, My Lord. She cannot help herself but be attracted to men since ten years old. Every possible scrape she has been in.... without thought for the consequences. The consequence does not occur to her.

My husband thought to place her at Shaftesbury as a haven for her since we appear to be unable to guide her ways. She is wilful, disobedient but simply an innocent in a world she fails to fully understand."

"That is not my question, Mistress Keylewey."

There was silence for a moment as the Abbot decided how to proceed. He felt his face becoming hot with embarrassment at having to ask such questions of a woman. Mistress Keylewey folded her hands in her lap and waited. She would not offer help or refreshments…. she had privately little regard for this Abbot standing in her house, who seemed unable to bring himself to ask the important questions.

"Seek out Sir Tobias, if you wish to know the details," Mistress Keylewey told him, suddenly tired of the encounter. "He has interviewed Winifrith and taken all the details of her ordeal. If you desire the sordid story he will be able to give it to you, man to man. I am sorry my husband is not here to deal with this."

She showed the Abbot out with little sympathy. He actually felt a little out of his depth for once as he stood uncertainly on the cobbles. He knew he must seek out Sir Tobias for the answers.

The answers, when they came, disturbed him, not because they cast doubt on Brother John, rather that they cast doubt on his own judgement of his fellow men. Penance would be necessary.

Sir Tobias had fortuitously called on the Abbey Infirmarian to enquire of the sick friar and to attempt to have gentle conversation with him concerning the original attack on Jenna and Isaac. Abbot Bradford found him there, crouched uncomfortably on a stool by the cot, his head close to Brother John to help him hear the laboured words of the Brother.

Brother Francis hovered anxiously in the background, flustered by the sudden presence of the Abbot, and ready with medicants if necessary. Sir Tobias was annoyed at the intrusion of Abbot Bradford, creating a heightened atmosphere of strain for Brother John.

The Abbot settled himself in a far corner of the room, uncharacteristically quiet and submissive.

"We had reached the making of the hide in the glade..." Sir Tobias reminded the friar calmly. Abbot Bradford had to lean forward in his seat to hear the broken words, emitting unevenly from Brother John.

He learned of the hide, of Brother John's desire to record the forest creatures with his inks; he listened to the raw fear in his voice as he re-lived the masked men, naked and wildly leaping, gesticulating, screeching as they dragged their victim, trailing blood through the undergrowth....he heard with horror how the fire had consumed so much ...the finding of Jenna, bleeding heavily and unconscious....imagined, as he listened, how Brother John would find her body heavy as he attempted to carry her back to his perfect little ruined chapel, his haven of peace in the last days before he went to his maker. The care for Jenna and his fresh fear that the perpetrators would remember their second victim and return to finish their work .....Brother John was tiring fast.....Sir Tobias helped him adjust his pillows and sip from the cup Brother Francis had left. Brother John's face was etched now with lines of pain as he recalled the events after Ezekiel and William had carried Jenna to Shaftesbury. On his return to his chapel, the wanton destruction of all he had held dear told him that he was now a marked man. There would be no peaceful end to his life; his only thought was to leave and make his way back to his Mother house in Ilchester. First, however, he would like to visit Sherborne. He described how he had met Winifrith near the main track to Sherborne, how he could see she had been violated and abused, how exhausted and confused she had seemed, and how in the end, she had tried to help him when he himself had felt the old familiar pain grip his chest, increasing, squeezing hard until he could no longer stand. The telling had exhausted him. He was spent, grey and trembling with the emotion of reliving the events.

Abbot Bradford stood, easing his back with one hand. Relief swept over him, but also an unaccustomed feeling of contrition as he realised that his first reaction to Brother John had been an accusatory one, a somewhat ridiculous one he now thought.....fearing that Brother John had violated the girl. He slipped out of the room unobstrusively.

Brother Francis was waiting outside, and timidly caught Abbot Bradford by the sleeve.

"Father Abbot, there is something I would like you to see." He took the Abbot to his apothecary store, and opening a small drawer, took out a faded piece of parchment. The illustration it held was of a small bird, intricate in detail and perfect in perspective. Abbot Bradford gazed at it for a brief moment.

"Where did this come from, Brother Francis?"

"It was tucked in the folds of the robes I removed from Brother John when I re-clothed him. It was damp; the ink has run, but what do you see, Father Abbot?"

"This must be the work of Brother John......it is very like the illustations in our own Missal.....illustrations made by a young friar....John Sifrewas...I believe he came from Ilchester."

Abbot Bradford's eyes widened in amazement as he wheeled about to return to the sick bed. Sir Tobias was about to leave.

"Sir Tobias, please ask the friar why he wanted to come to Sherborne."

Sir Tobias bent low to Brother John whose eyes were already closing in sleep.

The friar had heard the Abbot's words.

"It is nothing but sinful vanity. I thought to look one last time on the work I did as a young man on the Missal …..it was such a blessed time. It gave me such joy. I thought to gaze on it just once more."

Abbot Bradford's eyes filled with unusual tears. How had he come to judge this elderly friar so harshly! He turned away from the cot and studied the view from the narrow window as he composed himself.

"I will have it brought to you here," he managed to say with genuine humility.

Shaftesbury

Matthias and Ezekiel returned one last time to the Abbey in Shaftesbury to visit Jenna before returning home. Ezekiel was content that Jenna was being cared for and guarded with care; John Croxhale had offered to liaise with the Abbey on Ezekiel's behalf until he returned, which he planned to do in another week, but he knew he must return to his wife and sons and his other work in and around Sherborne for the moment. Jenna was making slow improvement. Ezekiel had talked with her about Isaac's death, but it had not been necessary to burden her with the details; she had wept silently, apparently not fully understanding or remembering. Ezekiel was very afraid that the head wounds had affected her in more serious and prolonged ways.

She was awake and sitting wrapped in a blanket by the bed, pale and rather tearful. Her shoulder wound was beginning to heal although still pained her considerably.

What bothered Matthias was the random pattern of killing, and the distance between the two towns. Maybe it was time the Coroner came to Shaftesbury and imposed some order on events. Their own bailiff and coroner did not seem to be able to do this. It occurred to him to wonder why. Why were the two men who should be investigating such troublesome, evil events apparently doing nothing...and where were they? He had not seen them at all on this visit. He said as much to Ezekiel.

"John Croxhale tells me they have proved to be a poor choice...there are better men in Shaftesbury. There should be two coroners but the bailiff persuaded the Abbess that one would be sufficient. The coroner's son is the clerk to both."

"And we could not find him, either," mused Matthias, suspicion hardening in his mind.

"Without Sir Tobias here I am unable to act as decisively as I think we should," Matthias murmured. He was much troubled now by these thoughts. If this was true devil worship it would be a matter of time before a further killing took place, however, it was possible that these events were the result of hallucinatory substances obtained from some source which mimicked devil worship but was proving to be addictive to the perpetrators. Which was it, and how should he proceed?

"I am going down to the place in Motcombe where I think Martin's old house was," Matthias decided. Ezekiel excused himself to revisit the home of his sister and brother in law one last time.

As Matthias jogged down the steep hill through woodland towards Motcombe he pondered on the possibilities running through his mind. John Croxhale had mentioned two young men following Winifrith.... possibly the coroner's son being one of them......might they have harmed Winifrith but been disturbed before they could complete their ritualistic killing? John Croxhale had appeared unpeturbed by Ezekiel's admission of Jewish descent and historic conversion, so that seemed to knock out any predjudicial reason. Might he find any evidence in the ruined house which he suspected was once the place Martin Cooper had returned to, belonging to his mother.

Motcombe lay at the bottom of a valley below Shaftesbury, a growing place already, one or two fine houses near the chapel of ease where there was a fine stone cross, already lichened with age. A cluster of smaller, simpler dwellings clothed the narrow track towards the old king's hunting lodge, but Matthias could see no burnt out house along here, so he turned back and followed instead the rough ground which led towards another cluster of poorer dwellings, each with a scrubby yard in front. The one on the corner was half ruined, with blackened lintel and roof truss collapsed and burnt. The next door place was also deserted...possibly due to the fire and the fear of fire spreading...such dwellings had roughly thatched roofs over the simple trusses and spreading fire was always a danger.

He looped his mount's reins over the tree on the corner and cautiously climbed over the rubbish which had accumulated in the overgrown yard. There was a broken wall with tumbled stones which had been arranged to form a sort of shield from the worst of the weather. Matthias wondered whether that was where Martin had crouched so long ago. If it was, no-one had disturbed that particular quarter of the place. The main room smelled very strongly of burning and something else he could not identify. There was sufficient roof left over this room to have afforded a place where things could be hung, and as Matthias reached up to feel the shelf his hands touched the smooth wood of something. His fingers followed the curves in the half light, round to a sharpened horn...on to a bulbous extrusion...the hairs on his arms stood up involuntarily as he realised he was feeling the outline shape of one of the masks.

With some gentle tugging, he managed to release it and brought it into the light. It was large, fashioned from carved wood and tree bark, dyed in hideous colours to give it staring, angry eyes and snarling jaws, slathering with blood. Although he knew this was man made, it made him shudder with a deep seated dread.

A slight sound behind him startled him, but not soon enough. The heavy timber came down crashing on his head, blackness engulfed him and he knew no more.

When Matthias did not appear back at The Swan, Ezekiel became concerned. He knew where Matthias had gone, the day light was fading, yet he took his horse and followed Matthias down the hill to Motcombe. It was dark by the time he arrived and he had no clear idea of the wherabouts of the house to which Matthias had gone. Despairing somewhat for his own lack of thought, he banged on the door of what he hoped was the priest's house. After explaining his mission, the young priest took him to where he thought there was a burned out house, first lighting a brand to enable them to see the way. The deserted house was silent and still in the night air...no sign of Matthias...no sign of his horse. No indication that anyone had even been there, except for the rank smell of burning and the odd unidentifiable smell which even Ezekiel did not recognize. Now deeply troubled, Ezekiel accepted the priest's invitation of a bed for the night and hoped the daylight would provide some answers.

Sherborne.

Richard Rochell and William Keylewey had arrived back in Sherborne after their business in London had concluded. They were elated by the success of their trip....they had crossed the Thames with some water boatmen and had hair raising tales to tell about the currents, the marvellous trade they had seen on the great river and the magnificence of the King's court – although they had not personally been inside the Royal Court. Servants had attended them, they had overseen the scribing of the warrant.....they had trouble changing their Sherborne money for silver acceptable in London, the values being different, but with the help of the scrivener they had achieved a satisfactory money change. Their excitement and pleasure in the telling of their tale were somewhat dulled when William Keylewey learned of the troubles of his daughter. He knew he must seek out the Coroner to ask for help in apprehending the culprits, for what if his daughter were to fall with child? It quite took the shine off his trip to London, following which all that was needed now was the King's seal on the document; they could then begin building.

Sir Tobias, however, had learned of their return and called on the Keyleweys the next day, telling them of his intention to ride to Shaftesbury and investigate the affair himself in the absence of any movement from the Shaftesbury bailiff or coroner.

He took William, his squire and Thomas his faithful scribe, first chaperoning Alice and Luke to Milborne Port. Alice was greatly enjoying Matthias' absence; she knew Matthias' methods and carefully followed his ways, but also enjoyed adding a little of her own ideas. She was careful to include the sons of Ezekiel, who had not been to school before, and who were both very shy. She was proud of the fact that she had not needed to call on Martin, and was pleased to find that Davy and Elizabeth accepted her as part of the establishment. There was only one flaw in her arrangements; she wished Matthias would unbend. Although there was no awkwardness between them neither was there any of the previous warmth. However, she was happy to be there.

Abbot Bradford had selected two monks to carry his beautiful missal to the infirmary. He did not delay; Brother Francis had indicated that Bother John was unlikely to recover, and Abbot Bradford had dispatched a messenger to Ilchester informing their Prior of the presence of one of his friars.

Brother John was propped up on pillows, pain still clutching at him cruelly from time to time. His face was still grey, lined with pain but his soul felt at peace.

Brother Francis moved a small table close to his cot for the Missal to rest on. It was a beautiful book, weighing nearly three stone in weight and with many pages, delicately lettered, illustrations gleaming from the pages with clarity and luminescence. Here was the story of Brother John's lifework. His fellow Brother, a monk also named John, had scribed the content, but he had laboured over the illustrations, and what illustrations they were! Saints, seraphs, angels, cherubim, popes intermingled with birds, animals, flowers, all meticulously drawn and coloured to perfection. From time to time and cheekily, he had even included himself and John Whas... tucked down in the margins among the gold lettering.

The two brothers who had carried the book between them regarded this sick brother with awe as he allowed his thin fingers to hover over the illustations....here a mistle thrush....a robin.....a skylark. Gillyflowers and lilies adorned some pages, whilst wily popes peeped round tendrils of leaves, interspersed with saints of many years ago....Saint Agnes, Saint Boniface, Saint Peter...the Christ child with his Mother.....was that Abbot Brunyng, peering round some intricate stone work? Brother John's lips moved in prayer and thanksgiving. He had not thought to see this again when he had felt so ill on his journey. After a period of time had passed, Brother John's eyes closed in sleep, and the Missal was returned to its room. A slight smile curved Brother John's lips as he slept.

Abbot Bradford felt such humility such as he had never felt before.

Shaftesbury.

In the light of morning there was still no sign of Matthias. Ezekiel was now seriously concerned, even more so when a young altar boy arrived to wait at mass, leading Matthias' horse. He had found it cropping the grass on the edge of the track, obviously turned loose.

He heard mass with the young priest and then requested that the priest keep the beast safe while he returned to Shaftesbury to seek help.

To Ezekiel's relief Sir Tobias and his party had just arrived at The Swan, and he lost no time in telling of the disturbing disappearance of Matthias.

Sir Tobias acted decisively; he called on the bailiff immediately, demanded that tything men be summoned and led the assembled party down the steep hill towards Motcombe. He insisted that the bailiff accompany them, and John Croxhale left the Swan under his wife's eagle eye as he too joined the party.

"If anything has happened to Matthias I shall feel personally responsible," he muttered to Ezekiel. "I should have followed my gut feeling and taken over this investigation. The bailiff has done little to help solve this unpleasant affair, and I am deeply suspicious of his lack of action."

"This is surely a fool's errand," he whined, overhearing his name.

Sir Tobias snorted derisively in reply. The fellow was as unattractive as he had been before, hardly less amenable and was unwilling to comment any further.

The place was as Ezekiel had seen it earlier, but a close examination of the ruined dwelling revealed a faint blood stain ...hardly noticeable against the scuffed earthen floor.

Sir Tobias and William looked carefully round, but there was nothing of note to see. The Coroner sent the three tything men in different directions with instructions to search for any signs of struggle such as dragging marks in the rough tracks, any sighting local people could add...but as the morning wore on, there was nothing. Matthias had disappeared. A pit of fear was developing in Ezekiel's marrow. He had become a friend to Matthias; as time went on he began to think of the treatment meted out to Isaac and his fear was making him feel physically sick.

"I think we should look to the forest, Sir Tobias," William volunteered.

"It is where Isaac was taken." Ezekiel said bleakly.

They left the tything men in the little village with the bailiff who was looking sullen and hostile again, with instructions to look in unlikely places now, spreading out further, even towards Kingsettle.

They went on foot, stopping every so often to call, pulling off the track to search thick undergrowth and aware that their feet were becoming bogged down in the marshy ground.

"Beware the lake..." William muttered, as they struggled through some sucking mud through the trees now beginning to burst into leaf with the lake just visible beyond. They could hear a dog barking, the first sound they had been conscious of since they had abandoned their mounts. The barking continued in bursts, and Ezekiel's strained nerves were taut with irritation lest the barking should prevent their shouting from being heard.

"Curse that hound!" he exclaimed, breaking away from the muddy track in exasperation. He strode angrily towards the sound of the barking to chastise the dog and send it on its way.

"Steady, Ezekiel. You'll find yourself bogged down in the marsh...it can be very treacherous here."

As the words were spoken, Ezekiel felt his boots sucked off. He floundered unsteadily, shouting with alarm. One boot was lost, the other filled with mud and William threw himself towards Ezekiel, who grabbed his arm for support. Both men fell into the mud, but it was less boggy where they had fallen forward and scrambling onto sounder ground, they both stood up, Ezekiel now with only one boot. Covered with oozing mud, wet through, coughing up the mud they had partly swallowed, they glared at the dog, now rushing frantically round in circles on the edge of the lake.

Sir Tobias glanced in the direction of the crazed dog. For a big man he was fast. There was something in the water which was annoying the animal. He prayed it was not a body. Had there not been tree roots at the edge of the lake just here it would have been a body. Matthias' head was lodged uncomfortably in the water, held just above water by the protruding roots. As the three men pulled him out it was obvious why he had not been able to haul himself out; his hands and feet were tied firmly together, and he was only just conscious. He must have been tied up, tossed in, but the haste of his captors had failed to ensure that he had been thrown far enough out to sink without trace.

William rolled Matthias onto his belly and pumped water out of his lungs. The movement of the water had meant that in his half conscious state, Matthias had been bobbing in and out of the water, and had swallowed copious amounts. He retched repeatedly as lake water was forced out of him. His body was icy cold. Another few hours and he would have died. Sir Tobias was the only one still dry after Ezekiel and William's tumble into the mud. He stripped his cloak off and divested Matthias of his wet garments, rubbing his limbs with his hands as firmly as he could to instil some warmth. William fumbled in his wet clothes for his knife and cut the bonds from Matthias' hands and feet, whilst Ezekiel knelt on the damp ground and helped to massage warmth into his icy body. Matthias, now wrapped in the Coroner's woollen cloak stirred, moaned and retched again.

"Thank the good Lord for a barking dog," William said, through chattering teeth.

The dog had now run away. The sport of attempting to retrieve something flung into the water had ceased.

"Back to the Swan as fast as possible. We must get some warmth into him urgently...the story can wait. I think we have only just been in time."

The journey back seemed interminable as they half carried Matthias between them. William and Ezekiel were still suffering from their fall in the mud filled marsh land,, and Ezekiel had not been able to retrieve his boot, so his ability to walk fast through the rough ground was severely hampered.

When they reached the place where their horses had been tethered and where they had left the search party of tything men, there were no men to be found. It appeared that the bailiff had allowed them to call off the search and return to Shaftesbury. Sir Tobias' face was dark with anger as they hoisted Matthias across the Coroner's own horse.

John Croxhale hailed them from the priest's house as they made their way to the track leading through the wooded valley towards Shaftesbury. He was leading Matthias' horse as well as his own but as he took in the scene he gave the reins of the other to William and cantered off ahead of them to prepare hot bricks and a chamber with a lit brazier.

Matthias, half conscious, couldn't stop shivering, drawing in air in frantic gulps as the party trotted up hill. He was slumped across the front of Sir Tobias' saddle, losing his grip from time to time and sliding sideways. Sir Tobias gripped him with one hand when this happened and slid him back onto the saddle. The movement of his horse made Matthias feel deadly sick; water dripped off his hair still although he was dry within the cloak. Ezekiel had Matthias' soaked clothes on the front of his saddle, and in this way, travelling as fast as they were able, they arrived back at the Swan.

Ezekiel dismounted first to help Matthias down from the saddle; Matthias slipped down and promptly disgraced himself by vomiting more lake water...

Master Croxhale had arrived before them; there was a room prepared with hot coals on the brazier, bricks heated for the feet, blankets to cover him. His wife was anxiously heating broth and both William and Ezekiel were apologetic as they trailed mud across the flagged floor, assisting Sir Tobias who was carrying Matthias now into the prepared room.

Sir Tobias' concern was to get Matthias warm again. They had no idea how long he had been in the lake, but it seemed unlikely that it would have been overnight; that he would not have been able to survive.

William and Ezekiel gratefully accepted dry tunics from John Croxhale, and his wife brought hot water for them with which to wash. A maid servant appeared to take away their muddied clothes and a pot boy brought broth, bread and ale.

Matthias lay with his eyes closed, shivering violently under the mound of blankets heaped over him. Sir Tobias raised him tenderly and spooned a little broth into him with his own horn spoon, but Matthias was unable to take it and dribbled it down his chin. Ezekiel looked down at this young man who had become his friend and knelt by the cot side. He wrapped Matthias in his own body warmth and lay close by him, gradually feeling the shivering grow less. The room was still, the warmth crept over the party. Eventually Matthias' shivering ceased and the men slept.

Sherborne.

Prior Nicholas from the Ilchester Friary arrived at Sherborne Abbey to bless this elderly brother who had opted to spend his final days in isolation and contemplation far from his Mother house. He and Abbot Bradford spent a short time in conversation and prayer before heading for the infirmary, a Dominican and a Benedictine walking together in harmony.

Brother John was lying still, his tired body temporarily at peace from pain due to the ministrations of Brother Francis. He had seen his goal, achieved his aim. If it was sinful pride he could live and die with that. He had loved his work on the Sherborne Missal and his merry relationship with John Whas. They had worked well together creating the beautiful thing, and had then each gone their separate ways. Since then he had travelled in the counties of Dorset, Devon and Somerset, teaching, preaching, helping the less fortunate and praying and worshipping with reverence. He was in truth a gentle soul, a lover of nature, an artist and in some ways a romantic, seeing beauty in wild life and able to commit the images through his pens and brushes. He had returned to his Mother house in Ilchester once or twice for spiritual refreshment and had once called in to the Dominican friary in Gillingham before finding what for him was the perfect place to spend his days... the half ruined cell at Cowridge in the ancient forest surrounding the old king's hunting lodge. He had always intended to return finally to Ilchester when he knew his days were nearly spent, but the events of the last month had robbed him of that aim. He would have to be content to remain here.

He opened his eyes, flickering from one figure to the other...black robes for the Dominican, grey for the Benedictine. He recognized Prior Nicholas and attempted to rise.

"My pride and vanity brought me here, Father; I should have travelled straight to Ilchester."

Prior Nicholas settled beside the cot, waving his fingers indicating that Abbot Bradford should leave them. His presence was calm, strong, reassuring.

Brother John received his benediction before Prior Nicholas left him to sleep.

A peaceful silence flooded the room when Brother Francis returned. His patient had no further need of him now.

Shaftesbury

Fresh anger filled Sir Tobias when he woke. Matthias was still sleeping, covered by sheepskins; Ezekiel had risen from the cot earlier and was now washed and dry again, ready for whatever the day should bring. William and Simon the scribe were breaking their fast in the weak sunshine outside the Swan.

Leaving Ezekiel to watch Matthias for signs of waking, Sir Tobias joined William to plan his next move. This had to be stopped; Whoever was behind this seemed to be curiously inept at completing their evil deeds satisfactorily.....two deaths each with one left to tell the tale.....an unsuccessful attempt to silence Jenna......an attempted drowning too hastily carried out.....and the attempt on Matthias' life had angered Sir Tobias more than he realised.

"That bailiff must answer to me now," he declared, grimly.

He strode towards the guild hall beside St. Peter's church, flung open the closed door of the bailiff's room and confronted the man as he slouched over his littered desk, gnawing on a greasy slice of bacon with hard black bread.

"No thanks to you, we found my man. Who gave you permission to call off the search?"

The bailiff stood up, dropping his bread as he did so.

"You forget that I am bailiff here," he blustered, wiping his hands down his stained jerkin. "The tything men found nothing. We could wait no longer; they have work to do....." he scuffed at the bread on the floor, trying to reach it. Sir Tobias put his foot firmly on the bread, sweeping the bacon slice off the table to join the bread on the floor. He became menacing as he confronted the bailiff.

"You run a sinking ship here in Shaftesbury. There are deaths, rumours of devil worship although I very much doubt that true devil worshippers would be as careless as some of these events have proved to be. Someone intended Matthias to die. Unfortunately it was not successful. Someone intended Jenna to die....neither was that successful. The young novitiate Winifrith escaped the clutches of the gaggle of incompetents who killed Imogen, also a young nun....Winifrith has been violated and abused since then....and the hideous death of the midwife Annestese leaves a grieving husband and young children. The wounds inflicted on these poor victims were hideous, particularly in the case of Isaac, but they are the vicious cuts of the inexperienced, crazed butchers who ape devil worshippers for some gratuitous means of their own. You are the bailiff here....why have you done nothing to investigate these things? All you have done is to arrest the wrong men... this is deliberate. Who do you think you are protecting? I warned you that I would watch....well, I have watched and been disgusted. The Sheriff will be informed, but first, we will get to the bottom of this pit of sludge for which you are bailiff. You will assist in my enquiries or I will have you committed to the castle dungeons."

The bailiff sat down cowed by the anger of the Coroner. He felt his bowels loosen, his bladder weaken. He tried to control his fear.

"So let's start with some answers," Sir Tobias continued. Simon drew out his parchment and quills and prepared to scribe. He cleared a space for himself on the littered table, following the example of Sir Tobias by pushing the welter of dockets onto the floor. He wiped the table with his sleeve before settling down to listen and record.

"Why did you not investigate the disappearance of Jenna and Isaac? What do you have against them?"

"I led a search for them when asked," a sullen reply.

"What do you hold against them? Answer my question. Why would they be picked out? They were attacked in the safety of their own home."

"I don't know."

"You said that they followed evil practices just before the forester rushed in with news of a death in the forest. What did you mean?"

"I've forgotten."

William fingered his sword and advanced towards the bailiff.

"You have no right to threaten me....I don't remember that far back."

"Only three or four weeks," Sir Tobias declared, acidly.

"Why did you bury the young novitiate when I expressly forbade it until you had made proper enquiries? "

"This town is not your town," a peevish response, made with bravado, clenching his buttocks against the churning in his bowels.

"I need to visit the coroner and his son. Take us to them."

Now his bowels would loosen. "I need the latrine.." William wisely followed him as he fled the room, loosening his points frantically as he ran.

A little later the bailiff had no choice but to walk to Cann with Sir Tobias, William and Simon.

The coroner's house was empty, closed and silent.

"Does the fellow have no work to do?" Sir Tobias asked, exasperated. William walked round the house, testing windows, rattling doors. They heard a whimpering inside, a scratching at a door. The bailiff turned away, fearful of another bloodied body. William put his shoulder to the door, manipulated the latch, the door creaked open a crack.

It was the barking dog.

Matthias woke with a splitting head ache. He tried to speak but found his voice had cracked hoarsely. Sitting up, he looked for his captors and found only Ezekiel.

"How did I get here?" he croaked. Ezekiel smiled.

"We carried you. You were in the Cusgarne Lake.. not the best place to be."

Matthias shook his aching head and felt for the gash on the back. It was sticky and sore. His hair had clumped and matted to the wound.

"I can bathe that for you, Matthias." Whilst he poured water to tend to the wound, Matthias tried to remember. "I went to the ruined house...I found one of the masks which Winifrith talked about...it was quite horrific...I don't know who hit me, but when I woke there were three men wearing masks, tying me up. I tried to hit out and grab one of the masks....but they were too far into tying me up...they left me there overnight. It was freezing cold." He coughed, trying to clear the rasping feeling from his throat.

"You brought up a lot of lake water. The retching is what has cracked your voice. It will come back. Take it slowly."

"One of the men returned when day broke. He was alone. He didn't have a mask so I could see that he was young....he had trouble carrying me but after dragging me through undergrowth he tried to toss me in but he wasn't very strong...I could touch the bottom but my hands were tied as well as my feet...." He stopped, recalling the icy water hitting him, the feeling of panic as he knew he couldn't help himself and the relief when his feet touched the soft mud at the bottom.

"I don't really remember much more....it was like a nightmare. I was colder than I had ever been."

"It took a long time to warm you through again, Matthias. They nearly killed you. You must have been in the lake for about four hours. Thankfully they didn't throw you in the night before. We would have lost you then."

"They were afraid you had discovered their identity."

"But I still didn't. Those terrifying masks....where on earth did they find them? They were frightening and solid...carved from wood and painted."

"That sort of thing can be found in markets abroad," Ezekiel told him. "There are several markets in Shaftesbury and many travellers....it is possible that they bought them here or in a nearby larger market... Salisbury, perhaps."

"But why? For what purpose?"

"To intimidate...to imitate devil worship....a game taken to excess....we need to put a stop to it....three deaths at least....burnings....horror brought to ordinary citizens....If you feel ready, we must find Sir Tobias and move towards an end."

Sir Tobias had the tything men out in force, searching for the coroner and his son and friends. The bailiff he committed to the care of the castle for the moment, uncertain whether he was truly involved or simply afraid because he had suspected and turned a blind eye. He was truly fired up now, angry that the good people of Shaftesbury appeared to have become the playthings of foolish men who were tampering with substances and rituals which had no place in their society. They had played with the devil and he intended to make sure they lost their game.

Matthias and Ezekiel caught up with the Coroner as he emerged from the Abbey, where he had informed Abbess Stourton of the chain of events. The Abbess had agreed to send a messenger to the Sheriff in Dorchester.

A watch had been set on the coroner's house at Cann, the dog taken by John Croxhale into the Swan, fed and tied up. Matthias wondered whether the dog would lead them to the coroner and his son if they set it free.

The dog was released, trotted obligingly round the market square, and then made off resolutely towards St. Rumbolts church, loping along happily, sniffing at rubbish in the path, cocking his leg against walls and hedges along the way. William kept the dog within his sight. At St. Rumbolts churchyard the dog went unhesitatingly to the far end and disappeared. William, after a moment's hesitation, followed in the same direction but first of all could see nothing untoward. A scrabbling sound at his feet revealed a cunningly concealed pit covered over with turf. The dog emerged and William knelt down and plunged his hands into the pit, finding two masks and a quantity of sacking, thin twine and a pot of some unidentifiable substance. It was nearly empty. He replaced the masks carefully, put the turf on top and looked for the dog, which was now standing forlornly, panting slightly, obviously disappointed.

William put the pot, the sacking and the twine in his scrip and returned to the Swan, where he found Matthias and Ezekiel waiting for Sir Tobias to return from overseeing the tything men. He was disappointed that they had little to report. They had searched as far as Enmore Green, Motcombe and the edge of the forest, even moving up towards Kingsettle. No trace of the three men were found. William showed the twine, thin enough to form deadly garrotte cords, and the pot of powder. The men smelled the sacking....definitely a thick, strange aroma but unidentifiable.

Ezekiel left to visit Jenna again, hoping that time had restored her memory a little more. Matthias accompanied him, William and Sir Tobias riding out to the castle to question the bailiff once more.

Sister Gratiana greeted them courteously, assuring them that they would see Jenna very shortly due to her priest wishing to visit her to say mass. He had requested privacy. He had only just now arrived.

Ezekiel didn't wait . He pushed past the astonished sister and was into the simple lime washed room where his sister lay, Matthias following.

The priest, on his knees by the cot, was offering Jenna the cup, elevating it above her head, and murmuring odd disjointed Latin phrases from the Mass. Jenna's eyes were closed in reverence as he had demanded.

Ezekiel in one fluid movement dashed the cup to the floor and wound his arm round the priest's neck, throwing him backwards onto the floor. Matthias pinned him down as Jenna started up in alarm, opened her eyes, looked fully into the face of the "priest" now lying on the floor facing her and screamed.

"That's the man who took us!"

Ezekiel and Matthias lost little time in disabling him, shocking Sister Gratiana with some very unchristian vocabulary.

The next few minutes were flurried and frantic. In the heat of the capture Ezekiel had failed to notice that the shock of seeing the man had restored Jenna's memory of the event. As the two men secured their prisoner, Jenna was pouring details out to Sister Gratiana .....how Isaac had seen the men with their masks and had unwisely confronted the coroner ....he had been offered money to ignore what he had seen..... refused......then the horror of the invasion of their house....how insane the men had seemed.....not like human beings anymore but crazed with drugs of some kind.....and then merciful oblivion.

Suddenly the peace of the Abbey was temporarily obliterated as the young man, the coroner's son, struggled, swore profanely, spat and clawed.

Sister Gratiana picked up the dashed cup from the floor but Matthias had the wit to command her to drop it.... "feed it to your rats!" he spluttered, for it was undoubtably poisoned.

The arrival of the Abbess restored a sense of calm. Sir Tobias had arrived to visit her again after his attempt to extract information from the bailiff where he had learned of the bailiff's suspicions regarding the coroner, once his friend. He was a weak character, who had thought to protect the coroner with a mind for future blackmail ....his tenure as bailiff was surely over.

The remaining task now was to discover the hiding place of the coroner and his son's friend.

"He will be close by, I surmise," Sir Tobias suggested. "We have searched a distance... no sightings of them.... there is a guard on his house....we need to look very close at hand."

"I can think of no safer place to hide than within the line of waiting pilgrims considering the presence of the fellow you have just apprehended," suggested Abbess Stourton with a flash of inspiration. "But I beg you, - no violence or undue disturbance in this Abbey."

Sir Tobias walked quietly into the assembled pilgrims, some chattering, some carrying gifts to offer. There were two nuns in attendance, keeping the line of supplicants moving. Sir Tobias took up a position from where he could see most of the people waiting. There was much camaraderie and good nature as well as some quiet reverence within the crowd. Sir Tobias watched carefully. Shortly he noticed that there were two men who continuously exchanged places with those in front of them so as never to reach the front of the queue. Snakelike he inserted himself into the line of people, excusing himself often to the person in front with a discreet whisper in an ear. The crowd was thinning a little. Those behind him now understood something was about to happen; it was as if the watching pilgrims held their collective breath. The arrest was skilfully executed. If those aware of the event had expected to be thrilled, they were disappointed. Sir Tobias simply gripped one arm of each man as he came within reach of them and eased them from the queue. His vice like grip brooked no nonsense, and the coroner and accomplice had no choice. William stepped forward to take one, the Coroner took the other.

The murderous tale was about to be laid bare.

Sherborne.

The cart bearing the body of Brother John left Sherborne for Ilchester with the blessing of Abbot Bradford, escorted by two monks and Friar Nicholas. Brother John had lived his life as a Dominican friar with humility and obedience, his only regret being that he had failed to reach his Mother house under his own steam due to his desire to see once more the Missal in which he had been so closely involved.

Mistress Keylewey and Winifrith watched it leave and turned somberly back to their home. Winifrith was healing slowly. She had learned a lesson from her frightening and humiliating experience, but how long that lesson would remain with her was doubtful. She was a genuine innocent, lacking in perception and purpose. Mistress Keylewey knew she still had the difficult conversation to be had with Abbess Stourton.... Winifrith did not wish to return to Shaftesbury, and it appeared it would be pointless to insist. Exactly what she would do now was open to question.

Abbot Bradford stopped them as they were about to enter their home. He bowed his head courteously to Mistress Keylewey and with some degree of diffidence offered to speak with the kitchen cook of the guesten house to procure a position for Winifrith if they would so like. Mistress Keylewey accepted his words without commiting herself, - it would be necessary to consult her husband and to visit Abbess Stourton to terminate Winifrith's novitiate. She was grateful to the Abbot for his thought. He, for his part, felt he had in some way continued Brother John's legacy of assistance and compassion. It was unlike him to be so thoughtful;

Brother John had left an aurora of humility behind.....
however unlikely it was to last, it was good to see it for
the present.

Lady Alice was becoming troubled by the continuing
absence of Matthias and now her father and William,
too. Davy, Elizabeth and Martin shared her anxiety.
There was no trouble with the school, - all was
continuing smoothly. Ezekiel's two boys were restless,
aware that their father was not yet returned, but as
Alice and Martin conferred together, they agreed that
the absence of news was disturbing. Martin had an
additional disappointment in that until Ezekiel returned,
he dare not risk any further progress or practice with his
prosthetic leg. He was fired up now to make some
headway with better walking but he could not do so
until Master Jacobson was home.

His task for Daniel de Thame was almost complete; he
felt encouraged by Lydia's support and hoped for an
increase in work. Alice implored him to be patient, - haste
would undo all the careful exercises he had carefully
followed on his stump every day, with Davy's help.

The party had been absent now for four days. Alice
wondered whether she should send Davy out to
Shaftesbury to make sure all was well. She worried that
her father had met with mishap; she couldn't bring
herself to admit that she was also terrified for Matthias.

Shaftesbury.

Sir Tobias had convened a makeshift court in the bailiff's
rooms. The coroner of Shaftesbury, his son and
accomplice were held with cords binding their hands.

The bailiff was not present, being still held in the castle. John Croxhale was invited to attend as witness; Abbess Stourton was also in attendance, and the masks found at St. Rumbolts were displayed on the table together with the pot of strange substance and the garrotte string. A crowd of townspeople had gathered to hear the end of this terrible episode, among them some Motcombe and Enmore Green residents. The atmosphere was heavy with menace against the three men.

The three men refused to look at the items, keeping their heads down, shoulders hunched, sweating freely.

Matthias spoke first, telling of the fires seen in the disused house at Motcombe by Martin. The villagers confirmed that the house had belonged to a woman of poor repute who had left with a tinker whilst her only son was away. Matthias was as sure as he could be that this was Martin.

Ezekiel was then called to tell of his finding his sister and her husband's disappearance, their house left in some disarray after apparently a disagreement with men who had called on them. He continued his evidence with the chilling description provided for him by Brother John of the massacre of Isaac...how he had seen naked men incoherent, they now realised, with strange drugs of some description dancing over a fire, burning clothes and hacking at the flesh of their victim. The listening townspeople fell silent, Abbess Stourton made the sign of the cross, Annastese's mother fell down in a faint. Neighbours held her and helped her out. Ezekiel's evidence continued.

"I am a barber surgeon. I have travelled on the continent; I have seen masks such as these in strange places, and know of substances often obtained in parts far to the

East of us and peddled by hags and bent apothecaries. These substances, mixed with crushed herbs and other potions can cause madness, hallucinatory visions, heightened desire, and a lack of reason while the effects last. I suspect that these three men discovered this, probably bought such a substance and found it exciting. They wanted power, it incited unnatural lust, violence, wild imaginings, horrid desires. It also stripped them of their inhibitions. They aped devil worshippers...might even have become such things had it gone on. My sister was with her husband when he was killed. She was injured and abandoned. The drug appeared to cause them to forget to complete their purpose; Jenna was left for dead with deep wounds near to her heart. I put it to you that these men are ignorant fellows who could not truly ape devil worshippers because had poor weapons and were always in a hurry to finish their terrible works, knowing that discovery would ruin them. This is your coroner," he poked at the bowed figure before them with his forefinger. "a man who was selected by some of you to order justice in this area. Not only is he a murderer and a violator of women but he has betrayed the trust of every man, woman and child in this place."

Ezekiel stopped, afraid that he had said too much. Sir Tobias nodded to Abbess Stourton who left her place as if on a pre-arranged signal and went to the door. The townspeople parted to let her through. She returned almost immediately with Sister Gratiana, supporting Jenna on her arm. She led her to sit beside the Coroner.

"Jenna," Abbess Stourton said, quietly, "Look at these men. Where have you seen them before?"

The room was hushed, breathless. Annastes's husband leaned forward to hear for himself what she had to say. Her voice was tremulous, little more than a whisper.

"They entered our house. My husband had accused them of evil practices and had reported them to the bailiff. The bailiff had not taken action but we hoped he would do so. We were intending to discuss it with my brother when he arrived from Sherborne, but they told us we should go with them to the bailiff again." Her voice weakened, her hands shook but she continued. "Isaac declined to accompany them as he did not trust the bailiff. They fought, but Isaac was no match for them, - there were three of them and only one of him. They left after spoiling my kitchen with their fighting." She wiped a tear from her eye. The assembled company had to lean forward to hear what she was saying.

"We left the kitchen to hurry to market. I was expecting my brother and we had wasted time... I thought I would right the kitchen when we returned... they were waiting for us just outside the chapel, hiding. We knew they were the same men but we had no chance....they dragged us down the hill and into the rough meadows. They stopped there, tied us up...there was nobody in sight...we were helpless. They took some drink from a phial and seemed to sleep for a while...when they woke they were different men...they had weapons which came from nowhere...I remember being dragged by my hair along the track towards the forest...Isaac was cut randomly at first....as they cut him the men shrieked and jumped....I was slashed in the shoulder...the blood ran into my eyes...the pain in my head made me scream out....it was where they had pulled my hair so hard...the man dragging me turned and beat me for screaming.....I remember seeing Isaac covered in blood...they hit me again....Please.. let me stop.....I don't remember any more."

Tears were now streaming down her face. Sister Gratiana glared at Sir Tobias.

"Enough, my lord Coroner, I think."

"Enough indeed," Sir Tobias said, icily. He stared at the three men. They cut a sorry sight now. There was no potion to embolden them, no person to speak for them.

"Why attack my young nun? Was her habit no deterrent to you?" Abbess Stourton spoke from her place beside Jenna.

"You holier- than- thou cow!" suddenly spat the third young man. He jerked his head up and spat in her face. Abbess Stourton gazed calmly at him and without taking any notice of the spittle running down her face she raised her hand in benediction over him. His lips parted in a snarl, his eyes snapped with passion. His voice rose to hysteria.

"What do you know about excitement, feeling alive, being in control? It was the most wonderful feeling and I would do it again. The silly girls thinking they were so holy, the self righteous midwife sneaking around in the middle of the night, the flirty nun who didn't want to go back to your nest of holiness....I was only sorry we didn't have the true excitement when we laid the silly girl on the ground and took our turns...we had no potion left until the merchant came to market again."

Matthias couldn't stop himself. He stepped up to the young man and slapped his face with a ringing slap, leaving a perfect imprint of his hand on the sneering face. The action stopped the man in his tracks. He suddenly seemed dazed, and held his hand up to his face, sobbing like a child.

"You fool, Edmund," Daniel said.

The Coroner concluded the court. The man had damned themselves. They would hang, all three of them.

It remained only to tie loose ends in the terrible events and make some suitable arrangements for Jenna. Abbess Stourton was willing for Jenna to remain within the Abbey infirmary until she was fully recovered. Her evidence had truly damned the men, who had started their killing spree only as an experiment in what the substance that Daniel's son and his friend had purchased from a shady apothecary in Salisbury would do. On discovering the extent to which they were able to journey outside their humble existence when taking the substance, they expanded; the younger man, the friend of Daniel's son, found the masks in Salisbury, in the same dingy apothecary shop dealing in spells and potions. They experimented with these, frightening a young maid who ran away. It was the first time they had taken the drug and worn the masks together and her fear had excited them.

Unfortunately, Isaac had seen them one day; they had not learned to be careful. He had warned them of the folly they were tampering with and had reported the findings to the bailiff. The bailiff was unwilling to act against the coroner, who could be an irritable man, and who also knew that the bailiff was not above pocketing part of fines and taxes for himself....a difficult situation.....and the bailiff and coroner had once been friends. Consequently the bailiff did nothing, and the three men decided that Isaac had to be taught a lesson. It was possible they did not intend the lesson to be as harsh as it undoubtedly was. They were inexperienced in taking such substances and had not anticipated the strength of the stuff. The leader appeared to be the friend, Edmund, who had become immersed in the evil practices associated with devil worship. It was he who had killed Annastese, acting alone when the strength of the drug overcame him, filling him with uncontrollable lust.

The abduction of Imogen was the work of the two younger men; they were unaware of Winifrith at the time as she had hidden herself. However, they knew she had returned to the Abbey and she put herself easily in their way by her own behaviour. They had not worn their masks on that day as they were hidden at St. Rumbolts in the pit, and so they had blindfolded her with sacking, used her as they wished and turned her loose, feeling she was well punished.

The information concerning the wherabouts of Jenna had reached them, and becoming nervous, Daniel had decided to deal with her, fortunately unsuccessfully. Sister Gratiana's swift intervention had prevented that; she was not a Shaftesbury lady herself and left the Abbey very rarely, so she did not recognize him. Angry and becoming reckless now, the three men roared through the forest to destroy Brother John for his interference. The total destruction of his place of safety and peace was committed by all three of them, without mercy. They were unable to decide in which direction he might have gone and were in haste to return to Shaftesbury to be seen as upright citizens, so neglected to search. They might well have found him if they had done so, for he was returning to his chapel by a different path.

The inactivity of the bailiff was their undoing. Sir Tobias became suspicious and took over the investigation

– and then Matthias disappeared. Sir Tobias became very angry and with his anger came action.

The coroner's son was preparing the Motcombe hide-out for another ritual with what was left of the current batch of their substance when Matthias discovered the masks, which had just been brought from St. Rumbolts. In a panic, Matthias was hit and restrained, left overnight in the disused house and in the morning the coroner's son lugged him to the lake and dumped him in, assuming he would drown. Everything had been done with indecent haste and incompetence.... except the macabre killings. Sir Tobias felt the young man was the ring leader, already a lost soul. He had shown no remorse, unlike Daniel and his son, although their remorse was heavily laced with selfish fear.

The Mayor of Shaftesbury now had to appoint two new coroners, and a new bailiff. He was appalled at the splinter of evil which had inserted itself into this gracious town, slicing even into the Abbey and was grateful to Sir Tobias for his intervention.

"Although had we had an honest bailiff, we should have stamped this out at the very beginning. We pride ourselves on our independence."

"Every town has its downside," Sir Tobias said, as they prepared for their homeward journey. Matthias was only partly recovered from his ordeal; he repeatedly experienced periods of extreme cold and shivering, and he would be glad to reach his own home. Ezekiel was content to leave Jenna at the Abbey and her neighbours would oversee the house for her until she was ready to return home, - then she would be able to take the next step forward. John Croxhale would keep a fatherly eye on her – he had been good to them all. Thus, they left Shaftesbury behind them.

Sherborne

The news regarding the Almshouse was positive. Richard Rochell and William Keylewey reported that the King was willing to grant the licence after various negotiations had taken place. The scribing of the document was under way, and by Summer they should feel confident enough to appoint an architect and a builder.

Dame Margaret had continued to be active so there was silver in the coffers and promises of building materials....wood....stone....and revenues from rents would keep the coffers full throughout the year. Altogether, a pleasing step forward for Sherborne.

The Keyleweys were visiting Abbess Stourton in the near future; the placing of Winifrith had not proved a success, and the dowry deposited there against her taking her vows may well have to be forfeited, but if the girl was so against it, there seemed little point. The Abbot had offered her a place with the lay folk in the guesten hall and they had accepted. If she was with child from her ordeal, they could not yet know, but they would have to deal with it if it came to pass.

Dame Margaret visited the babe placed with Mistress Amice and her husband; all seemed well there. A purse of silver had come their way for which they were grateful, but the gratitude was more for the fact that they now had a living child to love and nurture.

Sir Tobias and his party were tired and saddle sore when they arrived. Sir Tobias and William turned off first, jogging the last few miles of their way down to Purse Caundle. Matthias was next, he was glad because he was beginning to feel very tired. Ezekiel had to travel further towards Oborne, just outside Sherborne. He had much to tell and discuss with his wife.

Matthias reined his horse in before he reached home. The Spring sunshine lifted his jaded spirits as he gazed down the valley. He wondered how Ezekiel's sons had managed their few days in the school. He had discussed with their father on the way home whether he would consider keeping them at the school, - Matthias detected loneliness and shyness when he met them briefly before. School would be good for them. He was pleased that he had made a friend of Ezekiel; it felt good to have someone to talk with. It would be even better to have someone to share his life with, but perhaps that time might come. A slither of envy overtook him briefly as he imagined Ezekiel and Martha retelling their days to each other over a family meal. There would be no-one waiting for him quite like that, but he had Davy and Elizabeth, and for the moment, Martin. Lady Alice came and went; if he allowed himself to dwell too much on that incident he was tortured by not knowing whether he should have had the courage to ask her exactly what she was proposing, but he had lost his chance. It was gone.

Would he tell her about his near drowning? He thought not, - it was too dramatic, too like asking for sympathy, too like letting her into his life and expecting her to show interest. No, he would not tell her.

Two Abbeys, two towns, two worlds. One had touched the other briefly. Each contained good people, bad people, rich people, poor people. Sherborne had experienced bad times; Shaftesbury had emerged from a nightmare of wrong doing. Both contained Abbeys which would endure for ever, pointing their followers to God, stones which would never betray the faith, despite the frailty of human beings. It was a truth to hold on to, so Matthias thought, as he turned into Barton Holding.

His household heard the hooves in the yard. Davy and Elizabeth were first out, wreathed in smiles of welcome, then Martin, hobbling on his crutches as he emerged from the barn, eyes lighting up at the sight of Matthias. But most of all, to Matthias' delight and surprise, was Alice, shepherding his scholars out to greet him, obvious respect and pleasure on their young faces. He really felt as though he had come home.

There was more to come. Although Matthias felt he had emerged unscathed from his near drowning, the next day he found it difficult to rise from his bed. He did so with an effort, stiff in all his joints and experiencing the violent shivering which had assailed him the previous two days. When Alice arrived with Luke to take her place in the school room she could see that Matthias was hardly fit to stand, let alone teach.

Alarmed, she sent Davy to fetch Ezekiel Jacobson, sorry she had to do so because he too would have much to tell his wife and lost time to make up. His boys were not in school today, but he arrived himself at Davy's bidding.

"This is a kind of marsh fever," he said, frowning as he piled furs onto Matthias as he lay on his bed. "It comes from lying in that dirty water for so long, swallowing muck, becoming cold…"

"Lying in which water?" Alice queried, worried by the unhealthy flush on Matthias' face. Her father had told her of the trial and the recovery of Jenna but had omitted to fill in the details of Matthias' ordeal. Ezekiel held nothing back. Alice was horrified.

"How should we treat him?" she wanted to know.

"I hoped we had prevented this; I warmed him by lying with him so the warmth came from my own body. Your father piled clothes and rugs onto him and we ordered hot bricks for his hands and feet. He must be kept warm....keep the room darkened and allow him to sleep. It will pass, but he may be weakened for a period of time. I will come again tomorrow."

Alice returned to the school room after organizing Elizabeth into heating bricks, making broth, finding more rugs for the bed. Her concentration wandered many times during the morning. Martin came in to the school room to help, allowing Alice to seek Elizabeth, enquiring after Matthias.

Elizabeth had observed Alice as a woman will observe another. She was hesitant to speak her mind, but when Alice moved restlessly from one side of the room to the other, and then paced back again impatiently, she spoke.

"Lady Alice, go and sit in the room with him. I think you care what happens to him. Forgive my forwardness; Master Barton has been good to us but he needs family right now. He does not have family any more. He adored his family. He has no-one to adore any more. I think you mean something to him."

The room was in half darkness when Alice entered. She heard the hoarse sound of breathing but it was interspersed with dry, racking sobs. Unaware of her presence, Matthias spoke her name over and over again between those shuddering sobs. He spoke of his loss of her, of the loss of his sisters, his parents, his honour. Alice knew she should leave but she could not bring herself to do so. So she sat quietly by the cot, waiting for the torrent of grief to subside. Soon, he fell into a troubled sleep without ever knowing she was there. She remembered that once she had wished for this, had wished that his reserve would break. Her wish was fulfilled....what to do now?

Matthias woke, a sleep born of emotional exhaustion. The terrible shivering had returned. Alice could hear his teeth chattering as the ague overtook him. She recalled Ezekiel's words, and without hesitation, she did what Ezekiel had done- she lay close beside him, cradling his shaking body in her arms, warming him with her own body warmth. The shaking eventually became less.

Matthias lay still, amazed at the closeness he felt, relieved that he could lie so still and feel so much at peace beside her. His mind felt purged. In his weakened state he found words which he hadn't dared say before.

"You should move, Alice. My shaking has ceased for the moment. I would like you to stay...actually, to stay for quite a long time, but for now you should move."

"I would very much like to stay for a long time, Matthias," Alice replied softly, hardly daring to move.

"Your father asked me what security I could offer you. Do you think marriage might be a good security?"

"I haven't had much good fortune with marriage as a security, but perhaps that was the man, not the marriage. I should like to try it again."

"What can you offer me?" This time Alice didn't disappoint him.

"I can offer laughter, love and body warmth when you shake!"

"I must remember to shake a lot then." Some tight band of restraint which he had not known was present eased itself from his heart.

"I did not mean to sound so cold when we made our business arrangement, Alice. I did not think your father would consider me as a husband. He was seeking higher things."

"No, he was looking for security for me. I would add companionship, love and warmth. What made you think you had lost your honour?"

Matthias was silent for a moment. He recalled the upper balcony where the young courtesan had given him more than just the information about Allard's death, his own unexpected urgency and her subsequent death. He shuddered involuntarily. If he and Alice were to be true companions as well as lovers then there must be no secrets.

"There was a price to pay for the information regarding your husband's death," he began. Alice put her fingers on his lips.

"I always expected there was," she said, "I heard William tell my father that you knew the girl found dead by the gates in Paris."

"She was a courtesan, Alice."

"I did not imagine she was a nun, Matthias. I have been a married woman with a soldier for a husband. I am scarred by Allard's betrayal, but strangely, not by chance encounters."

Matthias lay still, warmed by the closeness of Alice's body. Sweet relief flooded over him and overtook his inhibitions. Raising himself on one elbow he looked down on Alice and bent his head to gently kiss her lips.

After a while, she disentangled herself and straightened her skirts. Looking down on Matthias she realised he had fallen asleep in her arms, a refreshing, healing sleep.

Tomorrow would be a new beginning.

Author's notes.

The historical link between Sherborne and Shaftesbury is in fact very weak. Most of these events are fictional, although there are some truths blended into the story.

Henry VI was still dithering on the throne, ruled by his advisors, and the consequence of his weak reign will influence the next Matthias Barton chronicle.

There was an inn in Shaftesbury called The Swan. It was one of many in the town at the time and the landlord was called John Croxhale. The Abbess at the time of this story was indeed Margaret Stourton...... Stourton House stands near Stourhead House and gardens today, and the gardens of Stourton are well worth visiting. Margaret Stourton was obviously from a local Shaftesbury family of note. Moreover, there is historical reference to the "naughty" doings of the nuns in the Abbey during the previous abbess' time, which would undoubtedly have lingered on in Abbess Stourton's time. There are stories in Shaftesbury of nuns being able to leave the Abbey by various exits....no-one seems to know which stories are fact and which are fancy! The buttress wall of the Abbey is still in place at the top of the picturesque Gold Hill, and one has to imagine the area as one of the chief market places at the time. There were others; Shaftesbury would have been a busy little town – not as little as it is today, for there certainly were pilgrims converging on the Abbey as well as traders from many parts of the area and probably beyond. The Abbey is now ruined, but it is a beautiful place to visit, with a well preserved herb garden and the area well documented for visitors to explore. More archeological work is currently being undertaken.

Details of medieval Shaftesbury are rather slim. There is only one house of the period remaining. It is in Bimport, very near to where the original entrance to the Abbey would have been. A walk down the hill towards the area known as St. James will give the reader some idea of how Winifrith might have been terrified by her descent down the hill, heavily wooded and slippery underfoot, not having the benefit of tarmac!

The details of Gillingham Forest are well documented; Motcombe, Enmore Green and the old hunting lodge of King John are all real places, growing in size as the period of the time progressed. Enmore Green has springs from which the water needed by the ale makers in Shaftesbury and others was needed. Water was taken up to Shaftesbury daily by donkey using leather buckets and young lads as carriers. The inspiration for the cell at Cowridge came from a simple idea told to me by neighbours – the farm behind the cottage in which I live is the oldest house in Motcombe and has a priest's hole…..I converted that in my imagination to a ruined chapel….the area was called Cowridge…consequently it became the place to which Brother John had retired. There is still evidence of the name today…my cottage is called Cowridge Cottage.

Lightning Source UK Ltd.
Milton Keynes UK
UKHW010633231221
396134UK00001B/178